THE Marble QUEEN

THE Marble QUEEN

STEPHANIE J. BLAKE

Amazon Children's Publishing

The characters and events portrayed in this book are fictitious. Any similarity to real persons, living or dead, is coincidental and not intended by the author.

Text copyright © 2012 by Stephanie J. Blake

Amazon Publishing
Attn: Amazon Childrens Publishing
P.O. Box 400818
Las Vegas, NV 89149
www.amazon.com/amazonchildrenspublishing

Library of Congress Cataloging-in-Publication Data
Blake, Stephanie (Stephanie J.), 1969-
The Marble queen / by Stephanie J. Blake. ~ 1st ed.
p. cm.
Summary: Freedom Jane McKenzie does not like following rules, especially about what girls should do, but what she wants most of all is to enter and win the marble competition at the Autumn Jubilee to prove herself worthy of the title, Marble Queen.
ISBN 978-0-7614-6227-9 (hardcover) ~ ISBN 978-0-7614-6228-6 (ebook)
[1. Family life~Idaho~Fiction. 2. Sex role~Fiction. 3. Marbles (Game)~Fiction. 4. Contests~Fiction. 5. Idaho~History~20th century~Fiction.] I. Title.
PZ7.B56513Mar 2012
[Fic]~dc23
2011040132

Book design by Becky Terhune
Editor: Robin Benjamin

Printed in the United States of America (R)
First edition
10 9 8 7 6 5 4 3 2 1

For Sam—
for always

Contents

July 29, 1959

The Last Will and Testimony of
Freedom Jane McKenzie,
of 121 Lilac Street, Idaho Falls, Idaho

If I die before I wake, my marble bag is for Daniel Coyle to take. Except for the light brown aggie. He knows which one. That marble's for my other friend, Nancy Brown. I promised to give it to her because I accidentally broke her ballerina music box last week, and now it has to be glued so her grandma won't know it was broken.

Signed,
Freedom Jane McKenzie

P.S. Daniel CANNOT have the blue taw, either. No matter what he says, it's for Higgie.
P.P.S. I mean it!!!

Chapter One

Taking a Stand

AUGUST 3, 1959

My mama, Mrs. Wilhelmina Anne McKenzie, was cutting up a chicken. And thinking back on it, I shouldn't have bothered her at all. Sometimes my mouth goes off, and I can't help myself. You know how you'll ask your mama about something, and she doesn't say anything for a whole minute, so you think she didn't hear what you said? Then when you ask for that something again, she starts hollering? Well, it happens at my house almost every other day, and I'm sure tired of it.

It was a regular summer afternoon. All of the windows in our house were wide-open, and I could hear the big boys playing stickball in the street. A heat wave rolled in through the ripped screen on the back door and swirled around the kitchen, from the brown speckled linoleum on up. Mrs. Zierk was plunking away on her piano next door. My annoying little brother, Higginbotham (Higgie for short), was sitting on the metal step stool in the corner, having a snack before supper, pretending he was invisible under the raggedy blue blanket that covered his dirty blond head.

Higgie always thinks he's invisible. His giggling was getting me riled. Instead of eating the peanut butter and honey sandwich, he was throwing pieces of it on the floor. Mama doesn't like it when we waste food, but she was too busy with supper to care. Even though Higgie's four, he acts like a dumb bunny most of the time.

All I said to Mama was that I needed a shiny new pair of roller skates because I'd lost the key to mine. Also, the wheel on the right one is kind of squeaky, on account of my leaving them out in the rain overnight. I scratched at a swollen bug bite on my leg while I waited for her answer.

A few minutes later, Mama still hadn't given me an answer about the roller skates. I noticed how round her baby belly was getting. I'm going to have a new brother or sister this fall. I've made my peace with it, but Mama hasn't.

She threw four thick chicken pieces into the black skillet, where they crackled and popped and practically danced in the grease. The smell of that fried chicken tickled my nose. My tummy growled with hunger. After she turned down the flame and put the lid on top, I tugged on her pin-striped apron. "Mama. Did you hear me? I really, really need some new roller skates."

I guess she'd heard me just fine, because she slammed a bowl of mashed potatoes down on the table and said, "You just had a birthday!"

It's true. I turned ten last week and got lots of neat presents. Aunt Janie and Uncle Mort gave me a little red diary. So far I've written my "Last Will and Testimony" in it. Nancy gave me a pink Hula-Hoop, and Daniel gave me a paint-by-numbers set. Mama and Daddy got me a Barbie doll.

Sure, Barbie is pretty and all. But I've only got the black zebra-striped bathing suit she came in. She's got teeny tiny shoes and gold earrings, and I'm afraid I'll lose everything. Mama was so proud when I unwrapped it. The doll cost a whole three dollars. I suppose I'm lucky to have it.

I guess I should've told Mama ahead of time that I wanted a brand-new pair of skates instead. We got my old skates at the church rummage sale for a nickel. They never really worked from the get-go, unless I'm on a steep hill. The only hill that's good for skating down is the one by Tautphaus Park, by the waterfalls, and I'm not allowed to go near Snake River by myself on account of that "terrible incident" last summer.

I could tell I'd upset Mama. She almost never wants to buy anything new. Her family was so poor she half grew up in an orphanage, although her parents lived in the next town over. It was the Depression, so a lot of people had hard times. Mama lived there for three years before her daddy came to collect her one day as if nothing had happened.

And now she's having another baby. But that shouldn't mean I can't get a Barbie *and* a new pair of roller skates, so I explained this ever so nicely. Mama sighed and brushed my hair out of my eyes before going back to the stove, where she complained about the lumps in the gravy.

She flicked a fly from her cheek and whispered, "You aren't getting anything new until Christmas."

"Christmas is four months away," I said. "I'd like to do some more roller skating before the summer is over."

Higgie giggled under his blanket. "Christmas!" he yelled. Then he pulled the blanket off his head and shoved his sandwich into his pink mouth. He chewed a bit and opened up wide, showing me the mess inside.

"You are disgusting," I told him. He pulled the blanket back over his head.

Mama simmered along with the gravy. Her wavy black hair was pinned up on account of the hot weather. Beads of sweat dotted her forehead. Mama had given up on her lipstick. Usually she's got on a thick red coating morning, noon, and night.

She banged the wooden spoon on the edge of the pot. "For heaven's sake! It's been one thing after another with you this summer. Freedom Jane McKenzie, find something you are good at and stick with it!"

How am I supposed to know what I'm good at until I've tried everything?

I put my finger up in the air and declared, "Mama, I *am*

good at something. I'm good at shooting marbles."

She handed me a stack of white dinner plates. "Marbles are for boys. Set the table."

Higgie popped his head out and said "Christmas" again.

"Hush!" I said to my brother. "But, Mama—"

"Not another word about it, Freedom!"

I hung my head. When Mama went to get the rolls from the oven, I poked my brother. His precious blanket fell on the floor. I stepped on it. That shut him up, except for the whimpering. He's such a baby. He put his fingers in his mouth, and as I went to poke him in the stomach, Mama caught me.

"Freedom!" She pointed to the bathroom. "Get yourself in there and wash your hands. I swear! Your hands are the grubbiest things I have ever seen."

I looked at my hands. I had a callus on my right thumb from shooting marbles all summer. I examined my nails. Black dirt was crammed up under each and every fingernail.

Mama narrowed her dark brown eyes and stared at my scrawny legs. I didn't dare look down, but I knew that my shins were probably filthy from kneeling in the dirt all afternoon with the boys at the ring. I'd played four games and won all of them.

I hoped Mama wouldn't notice the hole in my second-to-best yellow dress, where Daniel had pulled off the daisy pocket. He'd already won a cat's-eye and two aggies from me, and when I wouldn't give up a third aggie, he tried to wrestle me for it, ripping my pocket. I'd shoved him as hard as I could, yelling, "You can't wrestle a girl in a dress, Daniel Coyle."

He told me to go jump off a bridge!

Daniel lives across the street. We used to do everything together. Fun things like digging for fishing worms, skipping rocks at the pond, hunting for grasshoppers, and practicing yo-yo tricks. He's usually at our house more often than his own. He's been my best friend ever since I was in kindergarten and he was in first grade, but lately he's been acting kind of mean. The other day in the candy aisle at the drugstore, Daniel told me not to stand so close. He didn't want people to get the wrong idea. Whatever *that* means.

Of course, Mama notices everything. She snapped, "And what have you done to your dress?" as she followed me out of the kitchen. I skedaddled sideways before she could thump me with her spoon.

Daddy rustled his newspaper from the couch. "Now, Willie, leave the girl alone."

Seems my daddy, Homer Higginbotham McKenzie, is always saving me from Mama. I put my arms around his neck. He was still wearing his green work overalls and smelled of Schaefer beer and WD-40, with a hint of Old Spice. He might have been at work all day, but the ducktail part in the back of his hair was still perfect.

"That chicken sure smells delicious, Willie," he added. He gave Mama one of his big winks, and she stomped back into the kitchen.

I'll be starting fifth grade soon, and Mama has been going on and on all summer about what girls can and can't do. I never agree with her. *Never.* What's the matter with a girl shooting marbles? I'm talented. Daddy said so. He's the one who gave me the marbles in the first place.

In fact, almost all of the best marbles in my pouch were Daddy's when he was a young mibster. That's what you call a marble player, a mibster. And I'm one of them. Well, I am when the boys in the neighborhood let me play.

Daddy taught me everything I know about marbles.

He also gave me my unusual name. "Freedom is a good, strong name for a good, strong girl," he says. He also calls me Sugar Beet, but I'm trying to break him of it. My name fits me just fine, even though Mama didn't get to pick it out. She wanted to name me Ellen, after her dead mama, or Jane, after Daddy's sister; but Daddy argued that Jane makes a better middle name.

Mama says calling a girl Freedom is just borrowing trouble.

She doesn't know everything, though. For instance, when Aunt Janie gave me a pair of stiff dark blue jeans for Christmas last year, Mama said I couldn't roll them up because it showed off too much ankle. I wear dresses all the time, showing off my knobby knees, so I asked, "What's the difference between rolled-up jeans and dresses with bare legs and bobby socks? You can see my ankles either way."

Mama just said, "Don't get fresh, Freedom. You won't see Mrs. Kennedy wearing jeans."

It's always Mrs. Kennedy this and Mrs. Kennedy that. Mama claims I'll lose interest in marbles one day and be on to something else. I swear, I'm going to prove her wrong.

Daddy held up a page of the newspaper. "Look here, Freedom. They've announced the date of the competition." He read the words aloud: "'Twelfth Annual Marble-Shooting Competition to be held November fourteenth during the Autumn Jubilee. For ages ten and up. Sponsored by the *Post Register*. Entry fee: two dollars.'"

I jumped up and down. "I'm finally old enough to enter!"

Mama yelled from the kitchen, "We'll have to see about that!"

"And the prize is a hundred dollars!" I yelled back.

Daddy chuckled. "You can cut out the announcement after supper." He patted my arm. "Hurry now, Sugar Beet. Get cleaned up. I'm starving. And your mama is going to have a fit if supper gets cold."

I scrubbed extra hard with that slimy, red bar of Lifebuoy soap. I even rubbed my elbows and knees with a washrag until they stung. I thought about brushing out my stringy brown hair, but the knots were too big. Mama always complains about my sensitive scalp. I wish she wouldn't pull so fast with her poky hairbrush. She also says my hair wouldn't be such a mess if I'd stop "gallivanting around like a wild horse."

I counted three new freckles in the bathroom mirror

and decided it was time to take a stand. Everyone knows that girls are just as good as boys. Least that's what Daddy tells me. After I hung up the pink hand towel—nice and straight, the way Mama does—I came out to the kitchen and put my hands on my hips real important-like to make my announcement:

"I'm old enough to enter the marble competition this year. I've decided I'm going to be the next Marble King of Idaho Falls. You'll see."

Mama set down the platter of fried chicken on the table and pointed to my chair. "Sit, Marble King. Supper's getting cold." She tied a napkin around Higgie's neck. Then she went on, "I don't believe a young lady should be playing marbles with boys, especially against them. And furthermore—"

Daddy cut her off. "Let's say grace. I'm dying here." He put a chicken leg on my plate and grinned. Sometimes he looks exactly like Elvis.

Mama sighed. "I'll think about the competition, Freedom."

"Thank you, Mama."

After that it was kind of peaceful during our meal until Higgie said, "You can't be a king. Only boys can be kings."

"Fine, I'll be the Marble Queen then."

"You can't be a queen, neither," Higgie argued. "Queens are old."

He stuck out his tongue and rolled his eyes all the way

back into his head. All I could see were the white parts of his eyeballs. So I pinched him on the arm as Mama ladled fresh gravy onto Daddy's mound of mashed potatoes.

Now here I am in my room. So what if Mama sent me to bed when it's still light out? I didn't want that juicy chicken leg anyhow. I'm sure she threw the newspaper away, too.

But Mama had to do the dishes all by herself. So there.

Chapter Two

Higgie and the Worm

AUGUST 7, 1959

This morning Higgie and I had to go downtown with Mama so I could get some new shoes for school. All I know is that bringing Higgie along was a mistake. I tried to stay in step with Mama, but her heels were clicking on the pavement, and her black pocketbook was whipping against her side. Higgie galloped ahead. Mama was in a hurry because she had a doctor's appointment, and after that she still needed to finish cleaning up the house and bake a pie.

We passed the bank, the jeweler, and the drugstore. The street was nearly empty. A few cars were parked here and there. A man sat on a bench eating an ice cream cone. A stray cat streaked by. Higgie tried to take off after it.

Mama grabbed his collar just in time. "Higginbotham!" Whenever Higgie comes shoe shopping with me and

Mama, I never get a lollipop from the man who measures our feet.

Last time we got new shoes, Higgie squashed my toe with his dumb old stick pony. I cried, and Mama had to buy the saddle shoes that I was trying on because one got all scuffed up. I had wanted the penny loafers. The time before that, Higgie was leaning over in a chair and fell backward. He knocked over a display of shoe polish. Mama paid for five jars, even though we didn't get to take them home. I'll never forget the way the man's face got all scrunched up as he threw the broken jars into the trash can.

Right before she opened the door to the shoe shop, Mama tweaked Higgie's ear and told us, "If either of you makes a scene today, I'll take you out to the car."

I'm not sure why I was getting a lecture.

This time Higgie had already started trouble by getting his thumb caught in the car door in the parking lot. It's not my fault he wasn't out all the way before I slammed the door. Mama had said we needed to hurry. His thumb wasn't even bleeding, but Mama had wrapped her hankie around his hand and kissed Higgie's tears away, saying, "You'll be fine."

He kept repeating "My thumb is beeping" the whole time I was trying on shoes.

Finally, I got a pair of black penny loafers and a purple lollipop. Higgie got a red lollipop. I planned on asking Daddy for two pennies to put in the pockets of the shoes. When the marble competition comes around, I'll have at least two pennies toward the entry fee. That's if Mama lets me compete. I'm not sure why she's got to think about it so long, but I'm going to get Daddy to make her agree—somehow.

We hurried on to the doctor's office. When it was her turn, Mama told us to be good. "And keep an eye on Higgie," she told me sternly. I watched her walk down the hall with Doc Brooks and waited for Higgie to throw a fit.

But he didn't. The pretty receptionist with brown eyes had him under her spell.

"I'm Miss Hill," she told Higgie from behind her big desk. "Would you like to come and sit with me, Higginbotham? We can color." She held out a coloring book and a green crayon.

Higgie stood on one foot and cocked his head. "Nope." A few seconds later, he said, "Want to see my boo-boo?" He climbed up onto her lap and started to unwrap his hurt thumb.

Miss Hill examined it. "Oh, my. What happened?" Then she winked at me.

Higgie told her how I'd slammed the car door on his hand. She gave him a stick of Juicy Fruit gum from her purse and put a Band-Aid on Higgie's boo-boo. Then she drew a couple of stars on the Band-Aid with a ball-point pen.

It's always this way. Higgie can charm anyone when he wants to.

I stared at the closed door of the examining room.

Mama was taking forever. Waiting is hard work. I stared at the bright white floor and counted the tiles. I studied the paintings on the walls. One was of a tall building. One was of a bowl of flowers. I decided that the artwork didn't go with the orange plastic chairs we were sitting in. Or the brown carpet. My chair got more uncomfortable by the minute.

Still, I sat nicely, with my hands in my lap, while my brother took too many trips to the drinking fountain in the hall. Miss Hill couldn't stop him. The front of his shirt got soaked. He swallowed his gum. He drove his Matchbox car all around the floor on his hands and knees. He asked "When's Mama coming?" a hundred times.

At last Mama came out of the examining room. The minute Higgie spied her, he jumped up and said, "Hi, Mama! Look at my fancy Band-Aid."

Mama smiled weakly. Her face was flushed, and she tucked a wrinkled hankie into her pocketbook. "Did you thank the nice lady?"

"They've been perfect little angels," Miss Hill said. She put the crayons in her desk drawer and patted her platinum hair.

I rolled my eyes. No matter what Higgie does, people always say he's an angel. Probably because of his curly blond hair and blue eyes and chubby pink cheeks. I'm sure Miss Hill was secretly glad we were leaving.

Mama nodded curtly to Miss Hill, checked her watch, and grabbed Higgie's hand. "We'd better go!"

I asked Mama, "Is everything okay?"

"I'm gaining too much weight is all." She saw my worried face and smiled again. "I guess I'd better not have a piece of pie after supper tonight!"

I laughed.

She said, "Don't worry, Freedom."

Higgie wouldn't stop talking all the way home, asking why we couldn't go for ice cream, why was there a dog all alone on the side of the road, and why was the fence around the park so white?

When we got to our house, Mama set her pocketbook on the counter. "Why don't you two go outside and play?"

"It's too hot," I said. "Can't I lie on the floor in the living room and listen to the radio?"

I'd been good all day and I told her so.

She looked kind of tired. "Please go and get some fresh air, Freedom. And take your brother with you so I can have five minutes to myself."

"But what about my boo-boo?" asked Higgie.

Mama leaned down and kissed it. "Higginbotham, there's a bandage on it. It's time for you to toughen up." Mama pointed to the back door. "Go!"

I wasn't in the mood to play outside, especially without Daniel; but lately it seems like he's always got to mow the lawn or do chores around the house for his mama. Daddy keeps saying he's going to hire Daniel to help him fix up our house. The white siding is starting to chip off in big sheets. Mama says the house is falling apart. She might be right.

The sidewalk is cracked out front, the gate hinge squeaks, and the gutter is full of leaves and gunk half the time. Just last week Mrs. Zierk left a note on the front door about the "shabby exterior" and the "piece of junk" in the driveway.

Daddy says he doesn't have the time to work on it. Mama says it seems like he's got plenty of time to drink beer.

The minute we were out on the sagging back porch, Higgie ran off. I sniffed the air. I could smell a clove cigarette next door, so I peeked through the slats in the side fence. Mrs. Zierk was out in her garden, mumbling in Polish. Bees as big as silver dollars hovered around her wiry gray hair, while she used her broom to smack the grasshoppers off her corn stalks. She looks like a witch, but she's got the prettiest garden you've ever laid eyes on.

In the afternoons she sits on a chair on the back porch guarding her garden, watching everything and everyone with her all-seeing eyes. I feel like they're always on me, even when I'm in my own backyard. I decided to ignore her.

Mama poked her head out the kitchen window. "Freedom, can you pick some green beans?"

"Yes, Mama." She handed me the colander.

I wondered if there'd be any beans left in Mama's pitiful garden. The only things that ever sprout for Mama are green beans, tomatoes, lettuce, and onions. The rabbits have eaten most of the lettuce. The onions are puny, and the tomatoes never turn red.

Old Mrs. Zierk can grow just about everything God ever invented and then some.

Strawberries and raspberries. Bushels of lettuce. Big tomatoes. Beautiful onions. Cucumbers. And potatoes. Rhubarb grows wild in patches all around her backyard. Giant sunflower plants crawl up the side of Mrs. Zierk's house. She cans pickles and beets and all kinds of jam right in the backyard on top of a camping stove. The delicious smells drift around the whole neighborhood and nearly drive me crazy.

The ground was squishy and the air was so thick and muggy, I could barely breathe. I decided to dig for worms before I picked beans. Daddy has me collecting fishing worms in a coffee can for him. He gives me a penny for each one I dig up. So far we've got twenty.

I found the good silver spoon that I keep hidden under the rocks by the back step. It's the perfect spoon for digging. I made a teensy-tiny hole in the grass and put my finger down into it but didn't find a worm. I took a peek at the back porch. If Mama found me digging with her spoon, I'd need my Last Will and Testimony sooner than I thought.

Mama's been crankier than usual. Seems she's always yelling at me for something I did, or something I didn't do, or something she thinks I'm doing behind her back.

It makes me cranky, too.

The sun was burning my neck when I made another hole over by the garden gate. I pulled up a jagged rock and tossed it aside. Sure enough, there was a long, wiggly worm underneath. I bent down to pull the earthworm from the ground. He was so cold and gooey, I almost couldn't keep ahold of him. I wiped my fingers on my dress and pulled him up. I named him Jake and tucked him in my pocket.

It was time to pick those blasted beans for Mama.

I had about sixteen wrinkly beans in the colander when Higgie came around the corner of our house. The matted tail of his coonskin cap bobbed up and down. He was singing the *ABC* song while he whacked away at Mama's tulips with a stick.

"*A, B, C, D, E, F, G . . .*"

I waited for Mama to come out and start hollering about the tulips, but she didn't.

I had an idea. I took Jake from my pocket and kissed him on the head. Or maybe it was his tail. The earthworm curled around my palm, leaving a trail of slimy goo. I shivered in the hot sun. "Don't worry, Jakey," I said. "I'm not going to stab you with a fishing hook. Not today, my friend."

I should've put that worm in the can. Heck, I could've even given him a ride on the tire swing first. But I didn't. I decided to play Higgie's favorite game. I called, "Higgie!"

That dumb bunny came galloping toward me and swung the pointy stick right in my face. "Look, Freedom. Look at my magic wand!"

He must have gone back inside, and even though Mama told us to stay out, she'd tied a green-striped dish towel around his neck like a cape. He always pretends he's a magician. Or Superman. But we aren't supposed to play with sticks in case someone's eye gets poked out.

"Stop it!" I grabbed Higgie by his cape. "Do you want to

play Surprise with me or not? If you do, you'll have to close your eyes. No peeking."

After he squeezed his eyes shut, I threw the stick into the bushes. He wiggled around. There was dirt on his cheek, and his breath smelled like he'd been chewing on grass. I waved my hand in front of his face to see if he was peeking. He was. He giggled and opened one eye.

I poked him in the chest. "Do you want the surprise or not?"

"What do you have for me, Freedom?" He stuck out his pink tongue and panted like a puppy.

I thought I heard Mama coming. I checked the back door. No sign of her. "Here we go! Open your mouth, close your eyes, and you will get a big surprise." I made sure his eyes were closed. Then I dangled Jake right over my brother's mouth.

Next thing I knew, I had stepped in the mud with my brand-new penny loafers because Mama had nearly scared me senseless.

"Freedom Jane! What has gotten into you?" she hollered. "I can't believe I saw you feeding that worm to your brother! I never!"

"I didn't feed it to him, Mama. It was on his tongue for less than a second." Higgie was sputtering and making a terrible racket. "A worm won't hurt him."

Jake lay in the grass at our feet. Mama was still yelling. "And you're wearing your new school shoes, too!"

She led me by the arm into the house. The colander of

green beans got dumped over in the dirt.

"Go to your room until Daddy gets home, Freedom."

Maybe I'd gone overboard with that earthworm, but Higgie had *begged* me for a surprise. Jake was all I had.

When Daddy got home, he agreed with Mama. I had to stay in my room for the rest of the night.

Mama brought me a peanut butter sandwich. "I'm sorry," I told her. "I am really sorry."

Before she closed my bedroom door, she said, "There are consequences, Freedom. You need to start thinking about these kinds of things *before* you do them."

See, the problem is, I get these kinds of ideas all the time. It's from my "active imagination." My fourth-grade teacher, Miss Birney, wrote that on my report card.

I ate the sandwich for supper alone on my bed, not the least bit sad about missing out on liver and onions. Or the wrinkly green beans! But I've cried two buckets of tears over the banana cream pie Mama had made for dessert.

I'm going to starve to death if my brother doesn't stop getting me in trouble.

Chapter Three

Mama's Rules

AUGUST 11, 1959

Daddy's taken up bowling in a league. Mama says it's just another excuse to go out drinking with Uncle Mort and avoid his responsibilities at home. Every Tuesday night, right before supper, Daddy goes out wearing a freshly starched red bowling shirt that says HOMER in yellow stitching on the pocket, and he stays out until at least eleven. The rumble of the Chevy usually wakes me up when he comes home.

He doesn't even know how to bowl. It's making Mama foam at the mouth.

Before he left tonight, Mrs. Zierk came over and rapped at the screen door. When Daddy answered, she pointed to her giant white Cadillac at the curb. "Won't start," she said. Then she walked away without waiting for a response.

Mama said, "It's not our problem, Homer." She

followed him out to the yard. Higgie and I went after them. "You don't have to help her, you know. We don't owe that Commie a thing."

Mama is convinced that Mrs. Zierk is a Communist for three reasons: 1) because of the way Mrs. Zierk snoops over the fence without saying hello; 2) because she drives too fast; and 3) because she swears in a different language: Polish. (You can tell when she's swearing because she waves her arms and points at our house with her broom.)

I'm not exactly sure what a Communist is, but I know that Mrs. Zierk used to be a concert pianist, which sounds kind of similar. Now she gives lessons to kids and plays for funerals and events all over town. We hear that piano all summer because the windows are open. I don't mind, but Mama sure does. She complains about it to everyone we know.

Mama and Mrs. Zierk are always fighting about something. Most often it's on account of the burning bush that's in between our houses. It's called a burning bush because it's green during the summer and turns bright red in the fall. I think it's ever so pretty. Mama wants to chop it down because of the white spiders that live in it. Mrs. Zierk says she won't get rid of "the last thing my beloved husband planted right before he keeled over in the tomatoes."

Whenever Mrs. Zierk isn't around, Mama takes the big garden shears and cuts off a branch at a time. This morning Mama got caught. Mrs. Zierk stomped around on our porch bright and early, as mad as a wet cat, bawling Mama out.

Mama called her an "old crone" and slammed the door in her face.

If only Mama would stop cutting up the burning bush—and if only Daddy would stop chucking his beer cans over the fence—maybe that cranky old woman wouldn't hate us so much.

Out in front of her house, Mrs. Zierk already had the hood of the Cadillac up. She was peering at the engine on her tippy-toes like a ballerina, except she was wearing black witchy shoes. Her green-flowered dress was blowing in the breeze. I caught a glimpse of her lacy slip.

Higgie tried to get a look at the engine, too. "Get your sticky hands off my Caddy," Mrs. Zierk told him.

Mama said, "Come here, Higginbotham." Higgie went and hid in Mama's skirt with his fingers in his mouth. I sat on the step while Daddy pulled our car around.

Mrs. Zierk climbed into her car. Daddy got the jumper cables out of the Chevy's trunk and fixed the Cadillac right up. That old lady didn't even say thank you. After she revved the engine a few times, Daddy took the cables off her battery and let the hood shut. Mrs. Zierk nodded at Daddy, scowled at Mama, and drove away.

Daddy grinned and shook his head as he reached into the Chevy window to cut the engine.

"See what I mean, Homer," Mama said. "There's just no pleasing that woman."

Daddy checked his watch. "I guess I'm not going bowling tonight."

Now Mama grinned. Daddy leaned over and kissed her right on the mouth in front of God and everybody on Lilac Street.

"What are you making me for supper, woman?" he asked.

Mama practically whispered into Daddy's mouth when she said, "Spam and eggs." She squealed when Daddy let her go, and they chased each other into the house.

I wrinkled my nose—both for the kiss and the Spam. *Ick.* "Come on," I said to Higgie.

While we were eating supper, someone left half an apple cake on the back step, along with Higgie's Slinky and the baseball that had sailed over to Mrs. Zierk's yard last week after I showed my brother how to throw a slider.

I was amazed. Mrs. Zierk never gives our stuff back. She doesn't go to church; she doesn't give to charity; and the only time she ever turns off her porch light is when you knock on the door on Halloween night. Mama says Mrs. Zierk must be using up all the electricity in the world with that light.

Last year Daddy got the "harebrained scheme" (Mama's words) to build a bomb shelter in the backyard. He asked Mrs. Zierk if she wanted to pitch in some money and help. That way we could share it if the Communists bombed us. She said no. She said that we'd never even know if we got bombed because we'd disappear in a puff of smoke. That wasn't very nice.

Daddy ended up spending a whole weekend digging out

the bomb shelter with Uncle Mort. It's held up by some wooden beams. They hung up a single shelf, but so far nothing else from our house is in there. Not even a can of Spam. Higgie and I can't play in there because Mama's worried it'll cave in and kill us dead.

Mama held Mrs. Zierk's apple cake up to the light and sniffed at it. "I'd better slice it thin so we can check for razor blades."

"That lady doesn't mean us any harm," said Daddy. "You should be nicer to her. She's had a difficult time of it since Frederic died."

Mama snorted. "That man was a good-for-nothing. Like most men I know." She gave Daddy the eye.

If you ask me, Mama is too hard on Daddy. The other night Mama called him a good-for-nothing right in front of Aunt Janie.

Daddy *is* good at some things. He went to electrician school before I was born, but only for a year. He works as a small-appliance repairman, a part-time handyman, and an amateur locksmith; but I know he loves fishing best. Well, drinking beer *and* fishing. He's really good at fixing radios and toasters, and he's learning how to change the picture tube in television sets; but he could catch a fish in a snowstorm.

He also writes poetry at the kitchen table. Sometimes he reads it to me. And I always tell him I like his writing, even if I don't understand all of it. Daddy tries hard to get his poems published. Week after week, he spends four cents an envelope to send things to New York City. Sometimes he gets letters back. He always tears that creamy paper into pieces and throws the confetti into the trash can in the garage. I feel sorry for Daddy when that happens.

He does drink too much beer, though.

I try not to let it bother me, but it does. Mostly because it makes Mama and Daddy fight. Seems they only fight about two things: drinking and money.

But they aren't always fighting.

Late at night they'll dance in the kitchen to Johnny Mathis songs when they think Higgie and I are asleep. And sometimes Daddy brings home a bunch of wildflowers for Mama—just because. She cooks his favorite things. And she bakes something different for him nearly every day for dessert because he has a sweet tooth. Whenever they are walking someplace together, they'll hold hands.

The rest of the time Mama is mad at all of us for breaking The Rules.

She has a couple for me: Say "please," especially when you want something you can't have. Say "thank you" when someone gives you a present—even if you don't want it. Never say "ain't."

If Mama can't think of one of her rules, she'll say, "Mind your p's and q's, missy. Mind your p's and q's."

Some of Mama's rules are just for Higgie: Don't touch dead things on the side of the road. And don't you dare bring them home. Get your hand out of your pants. And your fingers out of your nose.

She has two special rules for Daddy, but he still forgets (he probably needs to write them down): Wash the grease from your hands before you sit on the couch. And put the toilet seat down. Actually, there's a third rule for Daddy: Don't come home drunk.

He's always breaking that one.

We ate up every crumb of that delicious apple cake.

Mama started clearing the dishes away. Daddy patted his belly and sighed. "I could eat a piece of that cake every day for the rest of my life and never get enough." Higgie burped.

Mama said quietly, "I wish I could get the recipe."

Daddy brought a platter to the sink. "You should ask her for it sometime, Willie."

"I wouldn't give her the satisfaction. Freedom, put the butter in the Frigidaire. Higgie, how on earth did you get all that food on your pants?"

Daddy and I pitched in and helped Mama clean up the kitchen.

When we were done, she hung up her dish towel and untied her apron. "How would you like to make some bubbles outside?" she asked.

I couldn't believe it. Mama never wants to do anything messy.

Mama said, "I found a recipe for bubble solution in the *Ladies' Home Journal*. And Daddy can tie some wire into circles so you kids can make giant bubbles out in the yard."

Higgie clapped his hands. "Thank you, Mama!"

We all went out to the backyard. The evening sky was like cotton candy: pink with low fluffy clouds.

Mama poured her solution into an old paint tray on the back porch. She handed me a wire circle. "You try it out first, Freedom."

I dipped the wire into the tray and took off running around the yard. A long bubble followed me. When I stopped, it broke off and floated upward. Higgie giggled.

Once I got the hang of it, I figured out how to pop my wire circle up and down to make smaller bubbles. Every time a bubble bounced around on the breeze, Higgie chased it until it popped. He got his own wire circle, and pretty soon tons of bubbles were floating up and popping all over the place.

Mama laughed and ran around with us. Daddy sat on the porch with a beer in his hand, chuckling every now and then, watching the whole show.

The show ended when Higgie knocked over the tray and spilled the solution all down the back steps.

Mama wasn't mad, though. She just took the wire circles and said, "Time for bed, Higgie. You, too, Freedom."

Her hair was a mess and her cheeks were flushed, but Mama sure looked pretty standing there on the porch in the breeze. She put her hand on her belly and got a funny look on her face.

Higgie and I stopped.

"What's the matter, Willie?" Daddy asked.

Mama put his hand on her stomach. "Do you feel it?"

"Feel what?" Higgie asked.

"The baby's kicking."

Daddy felt it and smiled. "He's going to be a football player."

"Or she's going to be a ballerina," Mama teased.

"I wanna feel," Higgie whined.

He stuck his small hand out, and Mama pressed it to her belly.

"Feel that, Higgie?"

Higgie snatched his hand away. "I don't want a baby."

"Freedom, do you want to feel it?" Mama asked.

I nodded and put out my hand. Mama's stomach was warm. She smelled good, like her fancy powder, and something else I couldn't name. Something sweet. I closed my eyes and felt a gentle nudge on my palm.

"Wow! Does it hurt?"

"It feels funny," Mama said. "Like bubbles."

I wondered if I was getting another brother. "A sister might be nice," I said. I didn't tell Mama that we could team up against Higgie.

Daddy said, "We'll know soon enough, won't we, Willie?"

Mama smiled and herded us into the house while Daddy stayed behind to hose the bubble solution off the steps.

Chapter Four

Daniel Calls Quitsies

AUGUST 13, 1959

Today was a terrible day for shooting marbles. It rained overnight, and the wind was blowing leaves and bits of trash into the ring. And know what else? Daniel is a quitter.

I snuck out of the house around two o'clock. After I helped Mama get a box of Higgie's old baby clothes down from the attic, she disappeared up there with a broom and a dustpan. Higgie was napping, so I figured it would be all right for me to go and play. But I didn't ask, because I'm still waiting for Mama to decide about the competition, and I didn't need a lecture about shooting marbles with boys.

The boys were gathered at Highland Park, like always. The circle was already drawn up over by the playground where it's nice and flat. The rest of the park is grassy. There's a pond in the middle where you can feed the ducks or have a picnic. Daniel and I have skipped rocks into that pond hundreds of times.

I had on my raggedy brown cardigan because of the weather. It's missing two buttons, it itches, and I can't stand it; but it's my play sweater. If I ever lost it, Mama would have a fit.

The boys hadn't been waiting around for me to show up, that's for sure. Even though I'm the one who makes the best circle. We play in a three-foot ring. That's why the game's called Ringer. You have to drag your foot around to make the circle in the dirt, and you should clear out sticks and rocks (but sometimes the boys don't take the time to do that).

Nancy was there, too, but I was the only girl squeezing herself into the game. Daniel, Anthony the Runt, the Meanie brothers, and Wally Biscotti started arguing because Daniel said it wasn't hurting anything to let me play.

"She's got some nice cat's-eyes," Daniel told them.

The boys gave in.

I smiled at Daniel real nice, but he still grumbled, "Oh, go on and let's throw lag already."

Daniel's daddy was a soldier who died in Korea. He's an only child. At night he used to come over and watch TV, but now he just sits on his front porch, watching people go by while he waits for his mama to get home from work. Mrs. Coyle is the head cashier at Kroger's grocery store. She comes over on her day off for a game of canasta with Mama. And sometimes my aunt Janie comes over, too.

When Aunt Janie brings along her Tupperware samples, Mama gets testy. She says that Aunt Janie is always looking to make a quick buck. Daddy says Daniel's mama can't afford Tupperware, or anything else for that matter, and that Aunt Janie should leave her alone.

Everyone says Mrs. Coyle's got a crush on Mr. Kroger, who's married and has about ten kids.

You'll get a fat lip if Daniel catches you gossiping about his mama.

"Hurry up and throw," Daniel told me again.

I can't shoot when my arms are covered, so I asked Nancy to hold my sweater.

"Sure thing," she said. I shrugged it off, and she folded it up and stuck it under her arm.

Nancy is the kind of girl who always has smooth hair and a clean blouse that's tucked in properly. That's why Mama told me to invite her over sometime for a tea party. I don't know if I want to. I don't like tea. And I don't like soggy cucumber sandwiches. And I don't especially enjoy playing nurse, or house, or Barbies, or any of those other boring things that girls are supposed to do. I'd rather play Ringer.

I pulled out my blue taw and threw it across the ring. Of course I won lag. We throw lag to see who goes first. Everyone stands in a line and throws their taws across the ring. If your marble goes the farthest inside the circle, you win. You play against whoever's marble came in second.

There's an awful lot of shoving at lag time. And the

Mooney brothers love a good fight. It's no wonder Jacob and Esau are named for the bickering sons of Isaac in the Bible. That's why I secretly call them the Meanie brothers. They are the look-alike kind of twins. Both of them have gray-green eyes and big feet. They also have the same crew cuts, except that Jacob has a cowlick.

Everyone groaned—except Anthony. Poor old Anthony Winkler can't shoot worth a penny. The boys call him the Runt because he's kind of thin and weak looking. I'm sure he'd rather read a book or build something with his Erector set, but he'd never have any friends if he didn't pretend to enjoy shooting marbles.

You have to bring your own marbles—no borrowing. Some kids have only a couple of chipped ones when they start out. I win a lot, so I've got loads. Your taw is your biggest marble. It's your shooter, the one you use to hit the other marbles. My blue taw was my daddy's. It's the prettiest thing ever made. It's got a burst of glass sparkles inside. I've got two other shooters, but I don't use them much.

There are all sorts of marbles: commies, fancies, creamies, aggies, cat's-eyes, and more. Cat's-eyes look just like a cat's eyeball with an oval swirl inside, and they come in red, blue, green, and yellow. Commies have nothing to do with Communists. They're just common—they aren't worth anything. I used to try to play with them all the time, but the boys won't let me anymore.

Daniel threw second best. He didn't act thrilled about

playing against me. He stood so close, I could smell the Black Jack gum on his breath. "Are we playing for keepsies or what?" he asked. Daniel's black hair was so long, I couldn't see his eyes. His jeans were too short, and his collar was even dirtier than usual.

"Do you want to?" I said as I took my share of marbles out of my pouch.

In Ringer, all of the players put some of their own marbles in the center of the ring—six if you won lag, seven if you were runner-up—and you set them up in a cross shape. When Daniel and I play marbles by ourselves, we almost always play friendlies. That way no one's feelings get hurt. But when we play at the park, we're forced to play for keepsies. That means if you lose your favorite marble, you can't cry. Not one tiny tear.

"Only if you'll play with your red cat's-eye." Daniel spat out his gum right over my shoulder.

I agreed, and set up the cross quickly.

Lately, the boys keep saying Daniel is in love with me. But I'm not sweet on him.

All I know is that Daniel was coveting my marbles.

Coveting is when you want your neighbor's stuff. I learned that in Sunday school after I tried on Linda Pratt's purple sweater. I took it from the back of her chair when she wasn't looking. I couldn't resist. It was oh so soft. Pastor Davis brought me up to the front of the class and told everyone I had stolen the sweater because of my sin of coveting. But I wasn't going to steal it, I swear.

The boys played rock-paper-scissors, and Wally lost, so he was named referee, which suited him fine. Wally Biscotti enjoys being in charge. His real name is Wallace Sachetti. He's twelve, but he looks like an Italian grandpa. His shirts are pressed and clean, and he wears thick glasses. He talks really loud.

As I knuckled down, Daniel cracked his new stick of gum in my ear.

The rule is: keep your hand in the dirt until your taw leaves your fingers—that's why it's called "knuckling down."

I ignored him and cupped my shooter. I have to get my taw nice and warmed up before a game. It goes farther that way. I blew on it twice. Then I blew on my thumb, too. For luck.

Someone behind me—probably Jacob—said, "Oh come on, why don't you go home and play with your Barbie?"

I didn't take my eyes off the ring.

When you play with the boys, you can't let them rile you. I kept rubbing my taw. If I threw it too far, it would bounce out of the ring, and I'd lose my turn. You get one point for each marble that you knock out of the ring until all the marbles are out. To get the perfect spin, you sort of flip the taw with your thumb, like you're flipping a quarter, with your fist balled up.

I knocked out three marbles with my first shot! I got so excited, I bungled my next one.

Daniel wiped his face and leaned in for his turn. I could tell he was nervous. His breath came out in puffs, and he kept running his tongue over his teeth. He knuckled down and knocked out my favorite red cat's-eye.

That's when Wally Biscotti pointed at Daniel's foot and yelled, "Hey!"

"What?" Daniel asked.

I looked down. The toe of his sneaker was just inside the ring. I pretended not to see. He's my best friend, after all.

I whispered, "Your toe."

No matter what, you can't put any part of your body—except for your hand—into the ring while you're shooting.

He stood up fast and dusted off his pant legs. "My toe wasn't in when I took the shot, was it, Freedom?"

I was willing to let it go, but not Wally. "You'll have to forfeit a creamie, Daniel."

Daniel tried to give me a creamie, but I put up my hands and said, "That's all right."

"Fine," Daniel mumbled, "take this one back, then. I know it's one of your favorites." The red cat's-eye winked at me from the palm of his dirty hand.

All of a sudden things felt different. The boys were laughing and poking each other.

I stomped my foot. "You don't have to give anything back! Just say I won, and we're even stephen."

I was ready to start a new game. We could have, too, if those boys weren't circling around, snarling like wolves. The only ones not saying anything were Nancy and Anthony.

"Take them all!" Daniel threw a handful of marbles on

the ground. "For the record, you didn't win, Freedom. I call quitsies."

Jacob shoved Daniel. "We don't play quitsies."

He held Daniel's arms behind his back while Esau rapped on Daniel's chest.

"Knock, knock—" Esau said.

"Who's there?" asked Wally in a high voice.

"A quitter, that's who," said Jacob.

Daniel was sniffling and blinking a lot.

Usually Esau is nicer than Jacob, but the only time they really get along is when they're picking on somebody else. And Jacob can turn on you faster than milk in the sun.

Nancy handed me my cardigan. "I'm going home." She tore out of the park like her hair was on fire. I probably should've gone with her.

Jacob wouldn't let go of Daniel. "Admit it. You're in love with Freedom McKenzie. So say it."

Daniel said, "I won't."

Wally whispered, "Girl lover."

Daniel wiggled loose. "Stop it!" He wiped his nose on his sleeve and started scooping up marbles left and right. Some of them were mine, but I didn't care. He grabbed his knapsack and stood up.

I heard a crack of thunder. It was going to rain again.

Wally did a little jig around the Ringer circle. "You gonna go home and cry to your mommy?"

Jacob said, "Naw, his mama's at work. He'll have to cry himself to sleep on his baby bed."

The Meanie brothers chanted, "Mama's boy! Mama's boy!"

Wally joined in.

Anthony stepped back. "Come on, guys, leave him alone."

Everyone else took turns shoving Daniel around, so I stepped in. I'm taller than Daniel by a tiny bit. I only wanted to stop the fight. "That's enough," I said.

And do you know what that rat fink Daniel did? He threw his last marble at me and yelled, "Why don't you go home, you girly girl?"

Wally Biscotti said, "Why don't *you* go home, Mama's boy! And take your girlfriend with you."

He threw a rock at Daniel.

Daniel began walking away. I went after him. Now Jacob and Wally were both throwing rocks. I saw one hit Daniel in the neck; but he didn't turn around, and he refused to run. I know he was scared, though. He was sweating. One rock hit me on the arm. It was only a pebble, but it stung. I wouldn't run, either. I glanced back at the ring. The Meanie brothers and Wally Biscotti were laughing and slapping each other on the back.

Anthony was walking behind us, shaking his head.

Daniel was crying, but I didn't say a word. The cut on his neck was bleeding. When I reached out with my hankie to wipe it up, he pushed my hand away. There wasn't anything else to do but follow him home.

When we got to my gate, he kicked at the curb. "I'm

getting too old to play with girls. My mama said so the other day."

I stared at him. "What's that supposed to mean?"

"It means we aren't friends anymore. Jeez, Freedom. Don't you understand anything?"

"Our friendship can't be over. We've known each other forever."

"Well, it *is* over. I can't have people talking about me. I'm not in *love* with you. I don't love anyone, except maybe my mama." He pushed the hair from his eyes and turned away.

I got this funny feeling in my stomach like it was twisting on itself. The wind whipped around. It began drizzling.

I thought about the times we'd fought before. When we argued over marbles. When I'd ripped a page in his favorite *Batman* comic book. And when he lost my lucky penny. We'd always made up at the end of the day. He even hugged me after one fight when I gave him a pack of colored pencils that I didn't want.

He shrugged and kicked at the curb some more. "I'm tired. And hungry. I'll see you around."

Daniel left me there. Alone.

I sniffed and tried not to bawl my eyes out on the street. Of course boys and girls could be friends. Weren't Mama and Daddy friends?

I stared at Daniel's house and waited for him to come back outside and apologize, but he didn't. Once Daniel gets something in his head, you can't tell him any different. I went on home. He'd change his mind the next time he wanted to watch his favorite cartoon, *Huckleberry Hound*. The Coyles don't have a television set.

When Mama asked where I'd been, I didn't have it in me to fight with her, so I said, "Playing jacks with Nancy at the park."

Mama smiled. "You should have brought her by. She's a good girl, even if her father is good for nothing."

It's true. Nancy's daddy owns the crooked car dealership on the edge of town. He's always flashing around money, smiling wide with his white teeth. He hit Nancy's mama one night outside the bingo parlor in front of half the town. They got a D-I-V-O-R-C-E, and people are still talking about it. I wonder which is worse, having your daddy die in Korea or having a daddy like Nancy's.

It wasn't until I was brushing my teeth before bed that I realized something that stopped my heart. When Daniel called quitsies at the ring, he was also talking about his friendship with me.

Chapter Five
The Big Zucchini

AUGUST 19, 1959

I was practicing a spin shot on the rug in the bathroom when Mama called me to the kitchen. There was a ham in the oven, and it sure smelled juicy. Her sewing basket was on the table. The button jar was out. She was trying to put a new button on one of Daddy's work shirts, only she couldn't seem to get the needle threaded. She licked at the white thread over and over with one eye closed. Mama is farsighted, which means the opposite: she's supposed to wear her eyeglasses when she does things up close like read or sew. Sometimes she's just too stubborn for her own good.

"Freedom, can you pull up the dead tomato plants? That storm last weekend nearly killed everything in my garden."

"Sure, Mama."

Mama jabbed the thread at the needle one last time and declared, "Gotcha."

Careful not to let the screen door slam against the house, I went outside. I stared up at the gathering clouds. It looked like another thunderstorm was coming. I stole a peek through the fence at Mrs. Zierk. She was standing in the shade, watering her rhubarb and fanning herself with her garden hat.

Mama's tomato plants were a raggedy mess. Every year she plants tomatoes, but they never seem to give much in the way of fruit. I pulled the wire cages out of the muck and started digging up the dried, windblown plants. The black dirt at the roots was cool and soft, and pollywogs scurried around under my fingers. I poked one, and it balled up fast. There were a couple of fat earthworms. I left them alone.

I saw a strange curlicue vine poking through the fence. What do you know! A giant green zucchini was nestled in under our dead tomatoes. It must have been growing quietly all summer. It was bigger than a watermelon. Bigger than a bread box. As big as a baby! I figured a flower had sprouted from Mrs. Zierk's vine and had turned into a perfect zucchini on our side.

I pulled up the last dead tomato plant, threw it aside with the others, and thought for a minute. My daddy loves to eat fried zucchini almost more than he loves drinking beer. It was harvesttime. The zucchini would die if I didn't pick it. Mama says wasting food is a sin, and zucchini is food—even if I don't like eating it.

I peeked through the fence again. A yellow jacket buzzed around Mrs. Zierk, and she was trying to whack it with her hat.

I decided that the right thing to do was to pick that zucchini. Mama would be so pleased.

The vine was tough, and I skinned the palms of my hands trying to get it up. The bottom of the zucchini was muddy from lying there all summer. I hiked the vegetable up on my chest and tried to balance it on my hip; but it was stuck to the vine, and the vine was stuck in between two fence boards.

Higgie had come outside, and he was having a jump rope contest with himself. I could hear him counting: "Four." *Thwap!* "Nine." *Thwap!* "Three." *Thwap!* "Six." *Thwap!*

I pulled again. Hard as I tried, I couldn't free the zucchini from the vine. I stepped back to rethink the situation. It was hot. Sweat had soaked my armpits. I had dirt on my clothes, and my hands were covered in mud. That zucchini was good and stuck. I couldn't carry it by myself, even if I got it loose. The answer was clear: I needed Higgie's help.

I called out, "Higginbotham! Get over here and help me."

Higgie's new thing was peeing outside, and he had stopped jumping and was squatting over a puddle he'd just made, watching ants drown.

"You'd better pull up your pants before Mama sees you."

Higgie ignored me and went off to pee on something else. I should have known he'd be no help. I heard Daddy's

Chevy pull into the carport. He had music on real loud. He came strolling through the back gate, whistling, with a transistor radio in one hand and a bag of beer in the other.

"Hi, Daddy, look what I've found!"

He came over. "Let me see what you've got there, Sugar Beet."

Daddy handed me the bag of beer and the radio and took out his pocketknife. He sliced at the vine with one quick motion. Then he picked up the zucchini and raised it over his head.

"Fried zucchini for supper!" he shouted.

I tried to smile, but suddenly I didn't think my plan was such a good idea. I didn't want to eat zucchini. I wanted the ham that Mama had been roasting in our oven all day.

Daddy went into the house with the zucchini while I followed behind with the radio and the beers. He was muttering, "Or maybe some zucchini cake or zucchini bread . . ."

When we got to the kitchen door, Mama grinned at Daddy like he was bringing her an armload of diamonds. I hid the bag of beer behind me so Mama wouldn't see it. Sweat rolled off my cheeks.

Daddy tried to dance with Mama while holding the zucchini. He took her hand and swiveled his hips and sang, "Maybe, baby, I'll have you for me—"

I set the radio on the counter.

"Turn down the music, Homer," Mama said, but she was still smiling. She flicked him away playfully with her dish towel. If you ask me, she needs to smile more often. She's pretty when she smiles. "Me, oh my! Where'd you get that zucchini?"

"Freedom grew it in the tomato beds," said Daddy.

Mama stared at me. She knew better than that. "Did you steal this vegetable from Mrs. Zierk, Freedom Jane?"

How come Mama always thinks the worst of people?

"Of course not, Mama. I didn't grow it, but I found it! Mrs. Zierk's vine poked through our fence."

Daddy took the beers from me and put them in the Frigidaire while Mama wasn't paying attention.

I thought Mama would be mad at me, but she was grinning. "Well, well. That old bat will have to share some of her summer bounty, after all." Mama must have been extra happy because she'd beaten Mrs. Zierk two times in one day. Mama had cut a branch off the burning bush that very morning.

Daddy decided, "I'll take fried zucchini, Willie." He kissed Mama on the cheek and reached for the newspaper on the table.

Mama said, "Freedom, wash your hands. I'm going to show you how to make Daddy's favorite treat."

Daddy turned the radio back up and got a beer.

I scrubbed my hands in the bathroom and wondered what game my brother was up to now. I'd be suffering in the hot kitchen with Mama and that blasted zucchini.

When I came out, Mama tied a clean apron around my waist. "A woman needs to be the queen of the kitchen if she wants to make her family happy, Freedom. You'll have to learn to cook sometime, and this is as good a time as any so you can help when the baby gets here."

I don't want to be queen of anything—except marbles. And truthfully, Mama is not that good of a teacher, but I held my tongue. I started thinking about that baby. Higgie and I already share the extra bedroom. Where was the baby going to sleep?

I must've been scowling, because Mama said, "Freedom, get me the skillet. And stop making that face. Babies are a blessing."

How could Mama read my thoughts? Still, she didn't look so sure herself.

Mama showed me how to sift the flour, but I pinched my finger in the sifter. I got to crack an egg, but she made me pick out the shells. She sliced up the zucchini with the big knife all by herself. She called me "accident-prone."

The skillet got so hot, the grease sizzled. I admit I was a tiny bit scared of getting burned. We dredged the zucchini slices in the egg and flour and fried them until they were crunchy and golden brown.

She set the plate on the table and called for Daddy, who was reading the paper in the living room.

He came in and opened another beer before nearly drowning his fried zucchini pieces in ketchup. I don't know how he gobbled them up right out of the grease like that. "Delicious!" I watched him get a third beer from the fridge. "I'll be outside."

Daddy let the screen door slam, and Mama flinched. I knew she was counting the beers, too.

"Go and see what Higgie is doing, Homer!" she yelled. "Now, for the quick bread," she told me.

Mama licked her finger and found a tattered recipe card in the wooden box over the stove. She got out the shredder and showed me how to rub the zucchini up and down the sharp points. That part was kind of fun. I shredded up the zucchini. She measured out more flour and sifted it.

"This was my mama's recipe," Mama said with a gleam in her eye. She looked happy and sad at the same time. "My mama could always make something out of nothing."

"Did she like zucchini?" I asked.

Mama chuckled. "She loved any kind of food. Even zucchini."

It never did rain. For the rest of the afternoon, while Higgie and Daddy played catch outside, I helped Mama bake zucchini bread and mix up a batch of zucchini slaw. The whole time, I wished I were shooting marbles at the park instead. I needed the practice.

By suppertime the zucchini was all used up, and Mama threw the ends in the trash. I was never so happy as when Mama told me we were finished cooking.

As we were doing the dishes together, I gathered up my courage and asked, "Mama, can I enter the marble competition this year?"

Mama paused for a moment. "I really don't think it's a good idea."

"But, Mama, I have my heart set on winning."

"I know you do, but playing sports with boys is just not ladylike." She smoothed my bangs.

"Please, Mama. Will you think about it some more? You don't have to answer me today."

"We'll see," Mama said.

I frowned. Everyone knows that "We'll see" is just another way of saying no.

"Come here, Freedom Jane." She pulled me close.

Neither of us said another word about marbles. I just let Mama hug me tight.

How on earth could I change her mind?

We ate the ham and potatoes for supper, with a side of gloppy zucchini slaw and a slice of nutty zucchini bread. I hate zucchini more than ever. It's green. It's awful smushy, and if you want the honest truth, it tastes terrible no matter how you cook it. If I ever find a surprise vegetable growing in our tomato patch again, I'll leave it where it is.

Chapter Six
Mama and Daddy's Kitchen Debate

AUGUST 28, 1959

Daniel never comes around anymore. He barely steps off his porch and won't even wave at me when I squeak by on my rusty skates. He just sits there reading a book like we've never met. I'll bet he misses *Huckleberry Hound*. And there's no way I'm giving back the *Superman* comic book he lent me right before he called quitsies.

His mama never comes around, neither, so she's probably mad at me, too. For what, I don't know. It might be because I got my kite stuck in their tree on Tuesday. And I had to leave it there when the lightning started. I heard Mama and Daddy talking about how Mr. Kroger's car was in front of Daniel's house for three hours in the middle of the night. Daddy said Mr. Kroger was probably over there relighting the pilot light on the furnace or something.

Mama smirked and said, "I'll bet."

I don't need Daniel Coyle anyway. I've got Nancy Brown.

Nancy and I went swimming at the YMCA pool on Wednesday afternoon. It was loads of fun. I didn't jump off the high dive like Nancy did. I didn't feel like it. Plus, it seemed awfully high up. Her red bathing suit sure is nicer than mine. I told Mama that I need a new one, but she said that summer is nearly over.

On Thursday Mama let me go to Nancy's house. I had to wear my best dress, the one with the blue cornflowers all over it. Mama put my hair up in blue ribbons. Nancy and I sat at a kid-sized white table in her room, while her mother served the most delicious store-bought heart-shaped cookies and sweet tea on fancy china.

I found out that Nancy is kind of bossy, and she still plays with dolls. She made me cart her Precious Baby doll around in the wheelbarrow while she put her teddy bear in a wire shopping cart. The doll's eyes open and close all by themselves—it's creepy, and I don't like it one bit.

We played with Nancy's collection of Barbies for over an hour, until I got bored to death. I asked if we could play jacks instead. Nancy said it is nicer to do what the hostess wants. I'm not sure that's true.

Mama says it's Nancy's turn to come to my house. But I'm not ready for that. I have only the one Barbie, and we'd have to include Higgie.

I tried getting into a game of Ringer today. The minute

Mama put Higgie down for his nap, I ran all the way to Highland Park with my marble pouch under my arm. The boys were starting a new game when I arrived. I was panting and had a stitch in my side. Daniel wasn't there. "Hey, can I throw lag?" I asked.

Wally Biscotti looked me up and down. "Nope."

"We've got a new rule: girls can't play," Jacob told me.

"Why not? Who's the ref today?"

Wally pointed at Anthony, who didn't say anything. He was counting a few marbles in his hand.

I asked, "Can I play or not?"

The boys ignored me.

I waited for them to change their minds until Esau said, "Not this time, Freedom." He was gentle with his words, but I got mad anyway.

I stomped away, but not before I said, "You are all a bunch of jerks."

They just laughed. "Go home, little girl!" Jacob called.

While I walked home, I had mean thoughts about those boys. By the time I got to Lilac Street, I decided it didn't matter if they wouldn't let me play. I'd practice shooting on my own, and at the Autumn Jubilee I'd show them a thing or two when I won all of their best marbles.

I planned on asking Mama about the competition at supper; but when I got inside, she was pacing around like a lion on the hunt, so I figured I'd better not. Somehow, Mama had found out that Daddy had skipped work again to go fishing with Uncle Mort.

She was looking for a fight when she served up Campbell's tomato soup and grilled cheese sandwiches for supper. That's lunch food according to Daddy; but he still wasn't home, and it was time to eat.

After supper Mama asked me to play in my room while Higgie got a bath. She put Higgie to bed when it was still light out. And for once he knew he'd better go right to sleep. Then Mama scrubbed out the Frigidaire from top to bottom, hosed down the driveway, and swept out the carport. I sat on the couch watching television with one eye on the door.

When Daddy got home, she started jawing at him before he could even wash his hands. He plopped down on the couch next to me. The smell of beer and cigarettes made my nose wrinkle.

"Put a coaster under that beer bottle, Homer. Why didn't you go to work today?" Mama asked.

He sighed. "Willie, summer's nearly over."

"What does that have to do with getting in a hard day's work? If you went fishing, why are you so late?"

"Mort and I got to talking about that darn Kitchen Debate, and time got away from me." Daddy patted my leg. "Vice President Nixon shouldn't have goaded Mr. Khrushchev in such a way. I'm telling you, we're going to find ourselves at war with the Soviet Union."

Mama went into the kitchen, and I followed her because I wanted a bowl of the tapioca pudding she'd made for dessert. But she didn't dish out the pudding. She went to the stove and put the soup back on. I sat at the table and waited. It wasn't the time to ask for anything.

Daddy came in and paced around the kitchen. "We're in real trouble here, Willie. Don't you understand how politics work?"

Mama said, "Shut the window. We don't need everyone in the neighborhood knowing that I've married a Communist sympathizer."

"That's not true," Daddy said, but he shut the window anyway. He opened another beer. "If you paid more attention to the news instead of what everyone's wearing in *Life* magazine, you'd know what I'm talking about."

Mama glared at him.

He sat down at the table with me. I didn't know what any of it had to do with our family.

"Do you want something to eat?" Mama put a sandwich in front of him.

He took one look at the tray and said, "Can't you see I'm having a beer? I need to *unwind*, Willie."

"From what exactly? Drinking all day?" Suddenly, Mama threw the tray of soggy grilled cheese to the floor and shouted, "I can't live this way anymore!"

She stormed into their bedroom. Daddy and I went after her. She bounced the cardboard suitcase onto their bed.

When she started throwing his things into it, he just

chuckled. He took a swig of his beer. A smile tugged at the corners of his mouth. "Give me a smooch." He reached for her.

Mama pushed past him. "You stink."

She opened a dresser drawer and took out some of his undershirts.

He sidled up to her and tried pulling her close, but her baby belly got in the way. "Come on, Willie. You know you aren't ever leaving me." Mama pushed him away.

His hip hit the corner of the beat-up oak dresser with a crack. The mirror above rattled.

Mama narrowed her eyes and pointed to the front door. "You're the one leaving. I mean it this time." She snapped the suitcase closed and tried to hand it to him. She pursed her lips.

I slipped out of the bedroom and sat on the edge of the couch, hoping I was invisible, not knowing what to do. Where would Daddy go? This was his home. I looked around. His books filled the shelves. Mama's knickknacks were lined up on the mantel. Their wedding picture hung over the fireplace. I saw that the round crocheted doily under the lamp on the side table had a stain, probably from one of Daddy's beers. The brown couch appeared more worn than ever.

It was *our* home.

I held my breath when they came out of the bedroom. Daddy stumbled through the kitchen doorway and came back with a fresh bottle of beer.

Mama opened the front door and put the suitcase down. "You are a good-for-nothing drunk. I should've listened to my daddy. I could have been a teacher. Instead, I ruined my life by running off to have a baby with you." She tapped her stomach. "I haven't learned my lesson yet."

Daddy stared at Mama for a full thirty seconds. The clock ticked them off one by one.

Then, in the quietest voice I've ever heard her use, she said, "Get out, Homer."

Daddy left the suitcase on the floor. He let the screen door slam behind him. He threw his beer bottle on the sidewalk, and the brown glass shattered. At last the Chevy screeched out of the driveway.

Mama yelled from the doorway, "You are going to crash, you fool!"

As the roar of the engine faded away, Mama fell to her knees and started to cry.

Mama never cries. When she's mad, she cleans.

Next thing I knew she was stacking Daddy's books and records on the driveway beside the suitcase. His bowling ball was out there, too. I peeked out the window, praying the neighbors didn't hear the commotion. After she put Daddy's favorite chair outside, Mama saw me in the window and yelled, "Freedom! Go to bed!" She was huffing and puffing. Her belly was too big to be dragging furniture around.

Mama went back to her bedroom and called Aunt Janie. The black phone cord snaked all the way across the kitchen floor and got jammed in the closed bedroom door. I could hear Mama crying again.

I put on my pajamas and lay on top of my bed. I couldn't stop thinking about all those things stacked up on the driveway.

What were the neighbors going to think?

Higgie was snoring in his bed. How could he sleep through all that fighting? I picked at the embroidered yellow daisies on my pillowcase. I got hot and opened the window just a crack. I lay back down and wondered why my daddy had to drink so much beer.

I must have slept some, because when I woke up, the house was still. I smelled cherry tobacco drifting through my open window. At some point Daddy had come home. I snuck out to the kitchen. He was sitting on the back step, smoking his pipe. The chirping crickets and the transistor radio were his only company. I didn't let him know I was there. I crept back to bed.

When he's upset about something, Daddy drinks beer after beer and leans up against the house, smoking his pipe, staring at the moon, thinking about important things.

Things that I guess my mama must not understand.

Daddy told Mama once that he's tired of the way President Eisenhower is running the country. He's afraid that Mr. Kennedy is going to be the next president and just make things worse. If you ask me, those are some awfully big things to worry about. Maybe Daddy should worry about smaller stuff.

As I began falling asleep for the second time, another thought occurred to me: That baby—the one that Mama ran off with Daddy to have—was me.

Chapter Seven

A Neighborly Chat

SEPTEMBER 1, 1959

This morning Mama told me to return Mrs. Zierk's cake plate. "I've had it long enough," she said.

Mama had washed it, put it away, and forgotten about it.

"Mama, she probably has loads of plates over there. Maybe, since she hasn't come for it, she wants us to keep it?" The beige plate has fancy scalloped edges. It didn't match any of our plain white dinnerware.

Mama held out the plate. "This one looks real special. I'm sure she's been eating nails, waiting for us to give it back."

I sighed and walked over to Mrs. Zierk's. I knocked on her door, hoping she wouldn't answer. I was bending over to lay the cake plate on the mat when she scared me half to death by peeking around the corner of her yard.

She was holding a rake filled with leaves. "What are you doing on my porch?"

I picked up the plate. "I only came over to bring back your plate. Mama said to tell you that she's sorry it took so long." I winced. Mama never actually said that. I shuffled my feet around. "The apple cake was real good," I added. "My daddy sure enjoyed it. He told Mama to ask for the recipe." That part was true.

Mrs. Zierk set her rake against the house. "Is that brother of yours with you?" Her gray bun stuck out from under her sun hat.

"No, ma'am."

She eyed me suspiciously. "Want some lemonade?"

I snuck a look over at my house. "Um . . . I'm probably not supposed to come inside."

She shucked off her gardening gloves. "Suit yourself. I'm thirsty."

I stood there holding the plate, thinking about cold lemonade.

She wiped her feet on the mat. "Are you coming in or not?"

I nodded.

When Mrs. Zierk opened the front door, I peeked over her shoulder. We stood there for a few heartbeats. I wondered if she'd changed her mind about inviting me in.

She opened the door all the way and said, "Either wipe your feet or take off your shoes."

I wiped my feet. The house smelled different from ours. Like old lady perfume. Cinnamon. Cooked green beans. And I don't know what else. My eyes went all around the room. I'd never seen so much stuff in my life. The walls were lined with paintings of butterflies. There were colorful doilies on every surface, even on top of the television. Books, teacups, framed photographs, and knickknacks were everyplace.

I leaned in to see what was in the big curio cabinet in the dining room. I was snooping, but I couldn't help it. The shelves were filled with thimbles and spoons from other states.

"I'm going to wash up," she said. "Pick a chair."

I noticed a single silver picture frame on top of her shiny black piano. It held a faded photograph of a girl who was probably my age. She looked very serious. A cluster of freckles dotted her nose. She was wearing a frilly white dress, and her hair was curled up like fat sausages.

I looked for a chair. There were three rockers to choose from. I sat down on the one that didn't have magazines stacked on the seat. The other had a pillow on it. I figured it was Mrs. Zierk's favorite, since her mail and a telephone were on the table next to it. A silky black cat jumped right up onto my lap and kept purring until I had to pet it. I looked around some more and patted the cat while I waited.

Mrs. Zierk came back carrying a silver tray with a pitcher

of lemonade and two glasses. She set the tray on the coffee table and groaned as she sat in the rocking chair next to me. "My old bones."

Her cat jumped from my lap and scampered from the room.

I pointed to the photograph on the piano. "Is that your daughter?"

She barely glanced at it before picking up her knitting bag. Mrs. Zierk pulled out a wad of yarn and began working her knitting needles while she talked. "No, that's me. I never had any children." She motioned to the tray. "You go ahead and pour."

I was careful not to clink the crystal glasses on the metal pitcher, but I was so nervous about spilling, I filled each glass only halfway. I set her glass on the tray. "I grew up in Poland," she said. "My family came to America when I was ten years old."

"Is that why you talk funny?"

She smiled a little. "I have tried very hard to speak proper English, but sometimes I forget. I am now Polish-American. It was my husband, Frederic, who had trouble learning English. God rest his sweet soul."

I thought about last year when Mr. Zierk keeled over. Daddy had sat with Mrs. Zierk while Mama called for an ambulance. Half the town went to the funeral. Mr. Zierk was a nice man.

I told her, "He always gave me a roll of Smarties when he saw me."

"Frederic got a kick out of your family." She sipped her lemonade.

I took a long drink from my glass. It was sour but refreshing. I didn't know if it was okay to set my glass on the coffee table, so I held it. "You must like playing piano a whole lot."

She set her glass on the tray and picked up her knitting again. "I was a child prodigy. Played piano since I was three."

"Sometimes we can hear your playing from our house."

Mrs. Zierk laughed. "I'm sure it bothers your mother."

"My daddy enjoys it. He likes to play harmonica. And sing with the radio. My mother sings, too, but mostly at church. Or when she thinks no one is around."

Mrs. Zierk paused at her knitting and stared me in the eye. "You know, I could teach you how to play piano."

"Mama says we can't afford it."

"Pish. Money. I have plenty of it. What if we worked out a trade?"

I set my glass on the tray and wondered what Mrs. Zierk had in store for me. I figured it would have something to do with hard labor in her garden. She surprised me when she said, "I have some strawberries in the kitchen. Would you like to help me make a batch of jam? My sister usually helps with all of the canning, but she can't make the trip this year."

"I don't know—I mean . . . I'm very busy right now. I'm supposed to be home practicing for the marble-shooting competition. I'm hoping to enter this year now that I'm ten." I don't know why I told her all that, but I couldn't think of any other reason why I couldn't stay and help her make jam except that Mama probably wouldn't want me hanging around Mrs. Zierk's house all day.

"Aren't marbles for boys?" Mrs. Zierk asked.

Somehow, I knew she was going to say that. She poured some more lemonade into my glass, but I stood up to go. "My mama is probably wondering where I've been."

She waved at me to sit down. "Don't get your shirt in a twist. All I meant was, what does your mother think about marble shooting?"

"Well, she'd rather I do something else more ladylike, that's for sure."

"*Hmph.* Are you good at it or not?"

Now, how could I answer such a question without sounding like I was bragging?

"Well, are you?" she pressed.

"Yes!" I said. "I *am* good at marbles."

I told her how badly I wanted to win in the marble competition.

Mrs. Zierk told me, "Where there's a will, there's a way."

I sat back down. "My daddy says girls can do anything. He said I could fly airplanes one day like Jerrie Cobb if I want. She's going to be an astronaut. I've never even been on an airplane. Daddy says it's only a matter of time before regular folks can buy a ticket to the moon."

I was rambling, but Mrs. Zierk didn't seem to mind. She just nodded and worked on her knitting. I could tell she was really listening to me. So I kept talking. "The other day my daddy came home all excited because a rocket took those pictures of the Earth from space. Of course, Mama said she'd believe it when she saw the pictures in *Life*. She never believes anything until she sees it in a magazine."

I had the feeling that I could tell Mrs. Zierk practically anything. Before I knew it I blurted out, "I have a secret." Mrs. Zierk's needles stopped clicking together. I leaned forward and whispered, "My mama has another baby in her belly, and I'm not sure she's happy about it. I'm not sure I'm happy, either."

Mrs. Zierk sat very still. Then her needles were clicking again. "That secret is for your mother to tell. You shouldn't talk about private family things, Freedom."

I knew she was right, and I started to cry. And do you know what Mrs. Zierk did? She put down her knitting and gathered me onto her bony lap.

"Babies aren't all bad," she said.

I sniffled. My nose was stuffy and running all at the same time. "They've been fighting a lot. My daddy is drinking too much." I flinched. I hadn't meant to tell her that.

"*Nie ma tego złego, co by na dobre nie wyszlo,*" she whispered.

"What does that mean?" I asked.

"Bad things often turn out to be good for you. You'll see."

I wiped my nose with one of Mrs. Zierk's embroidered hankies.

"Let's make some jam," she whispered. "Would you like that?"

I nodded.

Mrs. Zierk didn't hover over me the way Mama does. I carefully cut the top off each strawberry in one swipe with a paring knife. As the syrupy jam cooked on the stove, the air smelled so sweet, I wanted to take big bites of it.

After the jam had thickened up just right, we spooned it into jars. Mrs. Zierk put a dab of melted paraffin on the top of each one. I put the lids on as tight as I could. We boiled the jars in a pot, five at a time.

While the jam cooled, I had my first piano lesson. Mrs. Zierk was a patient teacher. I couldn't stretch my fingers to the right keys, but I learned a scale. Then I got tired, and I listened while she played a few songs instead.

She was playing the last few notes of a waltz called *The Blue Danube* when I heard Mama calling for me. "I have to go," I said.

Mrs. Zierk rose from her piano stool. She rummaged around in her pantry and came out with a jar. "Take some jam."

"Thanks. I had a nice time."

She handed me a jar of strawberry jam.

"Will I see you tomorrow? We can have another piano lesson."

I'd had fun making jam, but wasn't so sure about

learning piano. "I'll think about it," I answered.

"Maybe you can show me how to shoot marbles." Her milky blue eyes sparkled.

I jumped off the porch and ran to my own yard.

Mama was standing in front of our house. "You've been gone awhile. What happened?"

"Just having a neighborly chat with Mrs. Zierk."

"What could you possibly have to chat about?"

"You'd be surprised."

I told Mama that I'd had a free piano lesson. Mama sighed.

I frowned.

"Would you like a snack? Higgie is napping in the living room," Mama said.

We tiptoed around Higgie. His mouth was hanging open, and he had a tight grip on his ratty blanket. I'll admit he does look sweet when he is sleeping. Maybe I'll try to be more patient with him. It could be good practice for the new baby.

"I also helped Mrs. Zierk with a batch of jam."

She put the jar in the Frigidaire. "Probably has arsenic in it." Mama sat down at the kitchen table. "I've wanted to talk to you about the other night."

My face got hot. I sat down next to her.

Mama cleared her throat. "I shouldn't have said those things in front of you."

I had to know so I asked her, "What did you mean by 'running off to have a baby'?"

"Freedom, I was in college when your daddy and I met. My parents were very poor, but they had high expectations for me. The only reason I was in college at all was because I had a scholarship." Mama looked down at her lap. "Your daddy and I chose to start a family together a little earlier than expected, so I didn't finish my schooling."

I reached out across the table and touched Mama's hand.

"My parents never forgave me for that," Mama went on. "That's why you never got to meet them." She looked up at me. "Things haven't turned out the way I thought they would, but I love you, Freedom. You and Higgie. And Daddy. I know I'll love this baby, too. I shouldn't have said my life is ruined."

"It's okay, Mama."

"No, it's not," she said. "And I don't want you to worry. Daddy said he's going to try harder." She squeezed my hand.

The day after their fight, Daddy had bought Mama a bouquet of red carnations, and Mama had helped bring his stuff back inside.

The Chevy pulled into the driveway. Mama straightened her blouse. "Now, help me get a meal going."

"Thank you for telling me all of that," I said as she stood up.

Mama nodded. "You're a good girl, Freedom. I'm sure lucky to have you."

Chapter Eight
Gone Fishing

SEPTEMBER 5, 1959

Daddy shook me in the early morning hours. "Come on, baby girl. Get up!"

"It's still dark." I rubbed my eyes and tried to snuggle back under the warm covers, but he nudged me again.

"Let's go fishing, Sugar Beet. It's Labor Day weekend, and school starts next week!"

Daddy loves taking me to his special fishing hole. Mama says I'm getting too old to play with worms and sit outside all day with my daddy. She also says, "Teaching a man to fish only gives him permission to be a lazy bum."

That's not the way we learned it in Sunday school.

I had to get a move on, in case the fish were already jumping. I hopped out of bed, pulled on my brown dungarees, and did my business in the bathroom. There was no reason to bother with my hair, but I brushed my teeth fast and swiped at my sleepy eyes with a washrag.

Daddy popped his head in. "You want to go get Daniel?"

I wrung out the washrag and didn't look at Daddy when I said, "Nope. He told me he didn't want to come anymore."

Daniel used to come fishing with us all the time. Mostly, he'd sit in the shade and read a book, which irritated Daddy, but sometimes Daniel and I would throw sticks into the water and dig in the wet sand.

"His loss," Daddy said. He ruffled my hair and disappeared.

I felt bad for lying. But I wasn't ready to admit that Daniel wasn't talking to me.

I went back to the bedroom to put my marble pouch out of Higgie's reach. His fat foot was hanging out of the side rail on his bed. I made sure I didn't wake him when I passed by. Higgie can't swim, plus he gets tired and mean, so Mama always keeps him home. It was tempting to give his big toe a pinch; but he'd pitch a fit, and Daddy would leave us both behind.

That would make Mama happy. Of course, she thinks fishing is for boys. If we ever get an extra dollar around here, she's going to put me in ballet class so I'll learn how to carry myself like a "proper young lady." There's no sense in worrying about it. We'll never have an extra dollar now that a baby is on the way.

Once school starts there won't be many more chances to spend a whole day with my daddy. Uncle Mort would meet us up at the fishing hole, but I don't mind him, even if he acts as though he doesn't like kids. He just doesn't talk much. Probably because my aunt Janie talks a blue streak.

Uncle Mort has a big jiggly belly like Santa Claus, square yellow teeth, and a handlebar mustache. He wears Bermuda shorts year-round—no matter how cold it gets. He works with Daddy at the repair shop. Mama says he's always been a little "rough around the edges."

Mama was already up when I stumbled into the brightly lit kitchen. She was wearing her red-flowered housecoat and her worn slippers. Her hair was wrapped up in a pink hairnet. The kitchen was chilly and smelled like coffee. Well, coffee and ammonia. Mama scrubs the linoleum on her hands and knees on Saturday mornings before anyone gets up.

She was making our picnic lunches. The minute she spied me, she asked, "Did you go to the bathroom, Freedom Jane?"

I rolled my eyes. "Yes, Mama. And I tucked some TP in my pocket in case I have to go again later." I patted my pocket to show I really had a wad in there.

"Take some extra. Your daddy won't have any decent place to take you if you have to do number two."

I almost said something fresh, but I caught myself in time. I didn't say a single bad thing about the Spam she was frying, either. I don't know why we can't ever have turkey sandwiches on our fishing trips. Or roast beef. Mama worries about us catching worms from the mayo after it sits in the hot basket. So it's Spam and onions on Wonder bread. *Blech.* Spam tastes like old shoes after it's sat in wax paper all day. The grease always makes the bread wet.

"I won't need to do number two, Mama. I promise." Why does she have to mention the bathroom all the time?

Mama slapped some butter on a piece of bread. "You'd better bring your brown sweater. It might rain." She handed me an apple from the fruit bowl and finished packing the picnic basket with the sandwiches, some gingersnaps, and another apple for later. She also put in a Mason jar of water.

I wouldn't eat those gingersnaps if I were dying of hunger. I hate them. Mama won't buy Hydrox cookies anymore on account of Higgie—he licks off the cream and hides the stack of soggy cookies under the couch.

I twisted the apple stem. "A, B, C, D–" The stem broke off on D. "D for *Daniel.* Yuck."

"Please don't say 'yuck,' Freedom. Now, you be sure and eat that apple, peel and all, for breakfast. And don't go drinking Cokes all day. It's bad for your digestion."

Once Mama caught me throwing my apple peels in the garbage. She made me fish them out and eat every single one of them—even the brown pieces. I nearly puked.

Daddy came in with his tackle box and the can of worms I'd been collecting. "She can have a Coke or two, Willie. It won't kill her."

"It's going to stunt her growth. I know it."

Daddy winked at me, kissed Mama quick, and pinched her bottom. He grabbed the picnic basket. "I'll race you to the car, Sugar Beet!"

We ran out the back door.

"Be good!" Mama called. She came outside and added, "Don't let your daddy drink a whole six-pack before lunch. Homer, do you hear me?"

Daddy revved the engine and cupped his hand up to his ear. "Huh?"

I waved at Mama, but she stomped inside without waving back.

An orange-and-pink sunrise was coming up over the hills. I felt a smile cracking my cheeks wide-open. We practically flew down Riverside Drive to Hal's Bait Shop. I waited in the car and ate half my apple. When Daddy got back, he had two bottles of Coke for me and some cans of beer for himself. A box of fruit-flavored Chiclets peeked out of his shirt pocket.

He twirled a candy necklace around and around on his pointer finger. "Try it on, Sugar Beet," he said, tossing it to me.

All my life, I've wanted a candy necklace, but they cost a dime. Plus, Mama says it's not sanitary to lick something and leave it on your dirty neck. But Mama wasn't around. So I put on my colorful candy and decided not to lick it— too much.

"Oh, thank you, thank you!" I kissed his unshaven cheek.

Daddy grinned. "You're my girl." We pulled out on the highway in a spray of gravel. Daddy had one eye on the road and the other on the radio. "Open up the glove box and find my harmonica."

I popped open the glove box and found an entry form for the marble competition inside.

Daddy chuckled. "I thought I'd better pick one up."

"Does this mean I can enter?"

"I'll talk to your mama about it. You know she always has the final say."

"Do you think I could win it, Daddy?"

"Sugar Beet, you can do anything. Now, turn up the radio."

I fiddled with the dial. Our favorite Elvis song came on: "Teddy Bear." I know all the words. Daddy kept one hand on the wheel while he played his harmonica, and I sang along with the radio all the way to the secret fishing place along Snake River.

At the end of the song, Daddy curled his lip just like Elvis and said, "Thank you very much." I giggled. When he's in a good mood, Daddy is a regular clown. He's only serious about two things: political talk and his poetry.

He parked the Chevy on the side of the road behind Uncle Mort's pickup. Daddy popped a green Chiclet into his mouth. "Let's catch us some fish."

I grabbed our picnic basket and the Cokes. Daddy got his beers and took the tackle box, worms, and fishing poles out of the trunk. I scrambled behind him up the path to the river. Uncle Mort was settled at their usual spot in his yellow lawn chair. An empty blue-and-white one sat beside him for Daddy. I waved.

A nasty Camel cigarette was dangling from Uncle Mort's lip. Instead of greeting us, he said, "Haven't caught a thing."

Uncle Mort had spread out a red plaid blanket for me, and I took my place in front of them. As I admired the crystal clear water a few feet from us, I could hear the falls crashing on the rocks somewhere in the distance. I wished I were a shiny silver fish. I'd jump and dive under the bubbles all day and float in the quiet water all night without a care in the world.

Daddy was setting up my rig. "I'll need a bobber," he said.

I opened the tackle box and searched for a new red-and-white bobber. Daddy picked up a thick worm and held it out. It curled up in the breeze. "Want to try putting on the worm, Sugar Beet?"

I shook my head. I could hold a worm all day, but there's no way I'd be able to stab one with a fishing hook. I squeezed my eyes shut until Daddy was done. He told me, "The hook doesn't hurt the night crawler, Freedom."

I don't know if I believe him. Once I accidentally hooked Uncle Mort in the neck when I was casting. He cursed and carried on while Daddy plucked the hook straight out with the pliers without flinching. Uncle Mort had wiped at his eyes for about twenty minutes after that.

Daddy casts for me now. He threw my line out. It landed in the water with a plunk. He handed me the pole and reached into the paper sack for a beer.

When Daddy opened the can, foam shot out and covered the toe of one of my navy-blue Keds.

"Oopsie daisies." Daddy sucked up the foam that was overflowing from the mouth of the can.

"Take a load off, Homer." Uncle Mort motioned to the other lawn chair. Daddy sat down and pulled his faded brown fishing hat over his eyes.

A while later, we hadn't had a single nibble on any of our lines, and there were four beer cans at Daddy's feet.

The only sounds were the bugs buzzing and the birds tweeting. The sun rose higher and higher until it was directly above us. My neck got sweaty. I nibbled on my candy necklace and drank a Coke.

Daddy was snoring. I was kind of tired of fishing, but I'd never tell Daddy that. He might not bring me again. I had a big scab on my knee, so I hiked up my dungarees, picked it off, and flicked it into the water. I wondered what Higgie and Mama were doing. They'd probably gone downtown, and Higgie was having an ice cream sundae at the drugstore.

My stomach rumbled.

I opened the picnic basket. The Mason jar of water had tipped over. I set it on the ground next to me. I found the apple. I was so hungry I ate it peel and all without twisting off the stem first. There was nothing left to eat but gingersnaps and the sandwiches. I unwrapped a sandwich and bit off a corner of tough Spam. Mama had burned the lunch meat. I peeled back the bread to look at the mess inside.

Uncle Mort leaned over. "What you got there?" Another cigarette hung from his lip. I wondered for the hundredth time how he could hold it there and still talk. I showed him the sandwich, and he said, "Ick." And you know what he did? He threw that sandwich to the fishes and gave me one of his very own roast beef and mustard sandwiches.

"Thank you, Uncle Mort." I sunk my teeth into the soft bread and grinned.

"*Hmph.*" He blew a smoke ring into the air and took a bite of his sandwich.

I know that Uncle Mort saw some bad stuff when he was in the army in Korea. Stuff that Aunt Janie says we aren't supposed to talk about. I want to ask him if he ever shot anybody over there, but then I think maybe I don't want to know. He got shot at for sure, because there's still a piece of shrapnel in his leg.

After we ate, Uncle Mort pulled in my line and checked to see if the worm was still on. It wasn't. He added another one and threw the line back out. Daddy woke up just long enough to wolf down a Spam sandwich and gulp at his last beer.

About the time my own eyes were getting heavy, my line wobbled. I turned to Uncle Mort, and he smiled. "Grab ahold of your pole there, Freedom."

I held my pole tight, and Uncle Mort got the net ready. After letting the fish swim on the line a bit, I pulled that wiggly fella in all by myself!

Uncle Mort made me hold the fish a minute after he pulled the hook from its mouth. It was cold and slimy. "It's a trout," Uncle Mort said. "A tiny thing."

The rainbow scales glittered in the sun while the tail flopped back and forth.

"Do you want to throw it back or eat it for supper?" he asked me.

I stared that fish in the eye and squealed, "Toss it back!"

After Uncle Mort set the fish free, he patted me on the shoulder. "Good job."

Daddy slept through all the excitement. By the time the sun was low in the sky, I had caught three trout. I let them all go. They really weren't big enough for eating. Besides, I didn't want to get fish guts all over my hands.

Uncle Mort caught two ugly catfish. He put them on a stringer to take home for Aunt Janie to cook. Daddy drank a six-pack before lunchtime, but I couldn't tell Mama. That's why he didn't catch anything. He snored the afternoon away with a beer can sitting between his legs. His line wasn't even in the water half the time.

It didn't matter. It was the perfect day anyhow. Know why?

I peed in the bushes twice. Uncle Mort taught me how

to tie flies. Plus, I have a candy necklace of my very own—and an entry form hidden in Daddy's glove box for safekeeping!

Mama was right about carrying the extra TP. But I didn't tell her that, either.

Chapter Nine

Black Sunday

SEPTEMBER 6, 1959

I should've known it was going to be a black Sunday when Mama wouldn't let me wear my candy necklace to Sunday school. It's only missing fourteen candies, and it isn't even *that* dirty. Yes, the string is a tiny bit pink, but that doesn't matter to anyone—except Mama.

She wasn't in the best of moods. Daddy hadn't gotten up until she was putting the coffee on. Mama had stomped around, turned on all the lights, and pulled the covers off Daddy three times. He said he had a headache. She said there was no way he was staying home. "Nobody in this family gets out of attending church."

Higgie got into trouble because he tore the seat of his best pants on the fence sneaking out of the house while

Mama was bathing. He'd chased a cat up a tree. I had nothing to do with it. I swear.

I brushed some stubborn tangles from my hair. I put on a touch of cherry lip gloss that Nancy had let me borrow. I was slipping into my stiff saddle shoes when Daddy brought Higgie back to our bedroom. "Help him change his pants, Freedom. And hurry."

I pulled a clean pair from the dresser we shared and asked Higgie, "Why'd you go and do that?"

"I can't help it," he said.

"Yes, you can."

Mama hollered for us to get into the car.

Higgie stuck his tongue out at me.

I said, "Fine, you can button up your pants on your own," and slipped past Mama as she was patting her hair in the bathroom. I was wearing my candy necklace. I went outside. As I twirled across the grass, the candy bounced against my neck. I had on only one glove. The fingerless glove I'd made for shooting marbles was hidden in the bottom drawer of my dresser underneath the itchy red sweater that Mama gave me last Christmas. I kept the gloveless hand behind my back while I stood on the driveway waiting for Mama to come out and inspect me.

"You look nice, Freedom." She smoothed my bangs and stared me up and down. "But there is no way you are wearing that nasty thing to church."

I thought the necklace was just fine. The blue candies

even matched the blue cornflowers on my dress. But I realized I should've tucked the necklace under my collar until we got to church.

Mama said, "I already know you cut the fingers off one of your white gloves. I found them in the trash last week."

Oh boy.

I watched Mama tuck her golden thimble into her pocketbook. She wears that thimble on her middle finger during church. And if we act up, she taps us on the head with it. It's what the nuns used to do to her in school. I bet my head is dented under my hair because I've been tapped about a million times with that thimble.

I sighed and put my candy necklace in my purse before she could get it. She gave her own big sigh and put on her best white gloves. "We don't have time to find another pair for you," she said.

We walked to the car together. Daddy sat in the driver's seat. Mama poked her head in the window. "Homer, where's your hat?"

Daddy's head was resting on the steering wheel, and his black dress hat was in his hands. "Ah, stop fussing, Willie. My hat is right here." Daddy started the car. A sermon blared from the radio. He turned the dial. "We're already late, woman. Now git in the car!"

For once Mama closed her mouth and listened to Daddy. She opened the car door. He grinned, and Mama smiled back.

Higgie ran by, and Mama just managed to grab him. The knees of his second pair of pants were filthy, and so was his face. Mama dusted him off and licked her finger to rub the dirt off his chin. "Get in the car, baby boy."

I scooted in next to Higgie in the backseat. And we were off—"like a turd of hurdles, or a herd of turtles," as Daddy always says.

Once we got to church, I saw Nancy waiting for me by the front door. How could I miss her frilly pink dress and those shiny white Mary Janes?

"Hi, Freedom," she said. "Your dress is pretty."

My cotton dress looked shabby compared to hers, but she always has something nice to say. I wish I could be that way.

"Thanks. Yours is nice, too. Sorry we're late. It's Higgie's fault." I pointed to my brother, who was trapped in one of Mama's hugs. You'd think she was leaving him for weeks. An hour at Sunday school wouldn't kill him.

"Be good, Higginbotham," Mama said. "You, too, Freedom." She gave Higgie one last hug and off she went. Mama never misses her ladies' class, while Daddy stands around with the men in the fellowship hall for coffee.

We crowded into the fourth- and fifth-grade classroom. I sat between Shelly Sanderson and that snot with the purple sweater, Linda Pratt.

Wrinkly old Mrs. Peterson gave us a lecture on the importance of doing for those less fortunate. After the lesson we each had a cup of lukewarm lemonade and two saltines for a snack. I left my crackers on the table for those children in China.

As the congregation gathered together, I found Mama and Daddy near the back. It was hot. Mama was fanning herself with the program. One of the teachers brought Higgie over. "He was hiding in the baptistery again," she said.

Mama told Higgie to sit down. "It's time for worship," she whispered.

As usual, Daddy sat on the end of our row; Mama sat next to him; then it was Higgie; then me—even though Higgie always ends up on Mama's lap by the end of the service.

First, the congregation sang. Singing is my favorite part about going to church. Sometimes the prayers last so long my eyes need to close, but when the whole congregation sings, it's the best feeling. Especially when we're standing up. I can sing louder when I'm standing up. We sang every verse of "The Old Rugged Cross."

Mama has a beautiful singing voice, even though her breath could've used a mint or two. Daddy sang along for a few songs. He couldn't resist.

During the sermon, Pastor Davis went on and on about the seven loaves and seven fishes. Normally I don't mind talking about fishing, but that's not the part Pastor Davis was focusing on. He talked about how you have to do for others, and I'd already heard it in Bible class. I couldn't see around Mrs. Pratt's hat in front of us. It had a dead bird on top, which is just plain creepy, even if it is fake.

Daddy drew a bunny for me on the attendance card. Higgie and I played three games of tic-tac-toe. Mama held my hand during the prayer and squeezed it gently when I started to nod off. Still, Pastor Davis kept talking.

I lost my one glove under the pew, and my purse fell to the floor with a thud. I counted the panes of glass in the windows. I counted the number of black hats on the ladies' heads. I even counted how many people were sleeping: ten. Nothing helped. I was Bored with a capital B. I thought about marbles. I wondered when Daddy would ask Mama about the competition.

I decided to use my time wisely and pray about it. Isn't church the best place to ask God for a favor? I bowed my head and closed my eyes. *Please, God,* I said in my head, *let me enter the marble-shooting competition. Give Daddy the strength to ask Mama about it when we get home. And is it okay that I've made friends with Mrs. Zierk even though Mama doesn't like her? Amen.*

Mama poked my arm. She must have thought I was sleeping.

I leaned forward to peer down the row. Daddy was slumped in his seat. Mama was fanning herself and blinking like the sun was too bright. Higgie pressed up against my arm. He was playing with a penny. The seat was hard, and I couldn't stop moving my legs around. One foot kept falling asleep, so I tapped the pew in front of me with my toe, just enough to keep my foot awake. Pretty soon Higgie was tapping his penny on the edge of the pew in time with my foot.

I stifled a giggle.

Thump! I got Mama's thimble on the top of my head. I reached up to rub the spot, but Mama's eyes got wide. I put my hand back down.

Higgie kept poking me in the rib cage, so I finally reached over and pinched his leg. When he howled, everyone turned to stare at us. Pastor Davis didn't miss a beat. Mama's mouth was a thin red line. She reached around Higgie and yanked me closer to her. I was so close I could smell her cologne. I sneaked a look at Daddy, and he winked at me.

All was quiet in our row. Pastor Davis seemed to be wrapping it up. Suddenly, my hymn book fell to the floor.

I got the thimble again.

I stared at the *H* on the Holy Bible in the rack in front of me. *Hellfire* came to mind. Along with *Help*. I sniffed a little.

At last Pastor Davis was done talking.

The ushers were in the aisles. Mama and Daddy took communion. After everybody had a corner of a cracker and a sip of grape juice, it was collection plate time. Usually Daddy gives me a nickel to put in the collection plate. I held out my hand, but Daddy coughed and wiped his mouth on his handkerchief. Mama shook her head.

I got worried. The big silver plate was coming down our row, and I didn't have my weekly contribution for the missionaries in Africa. I turned to Daddy.

He whispered, "Not this week." I understood. We didn't have an extra nickel. I felt guilty about the ten-cent candy necklace in my purse.

The collection plate was passing Daddy's lap. I had to put something in it before it was too late.

Higgie had that blasted penny, and I wanted it. Not for myself, oh no—I needed that penny for Jesus. I intended to pry it from Higgie's hand. We struggled. Mama pasted a smile on her face and tried to pass the plate over my head to the lady next to us. I was holding Higgie's hand and tugging on his fingers. He wouldn't let go.

What happened next I don't rightly know. I had the penny in my hand. Then—with a crash and a cry—all of the quarters and pennies and dollar bills were on the floor at our feet. And the big silver plate was rolling down the aisle! Everyone was shaking their heads, looking at us.

I threw the penny on the floor right before Mama dragged me outside. As the doors to the sanctuary slammed shut, I smiled in spite of my troubles.

I was four cents short, but surely the Lord would understand.

Chapter Ten
School Daze

SEPTEMBER 8, 1959

On the first day of school, I wore a yellow-and-white gingham dress and white socks that were trimmed with a ruffle around each ankle. I had on my penny loafers. A shiny penny poked halfway out of each pocket. (Uncle Mort gave them to me for luck.) Mama had done up my long hair in a single ponytail with a white ribbon. I was feeling pretty grown up and ready for fifth grade. While walking to school, I had made myself a promise: I wouldn't be caught running wild on the playground. I would play quiet games with the girls in my class.

And I would ignore Daniel Coyle with all my heart.

Truth is, I was nervous, and I probably wasn't the only one. Seems we were all early, milling around, talking about our summer vacations. I didn't see Nancy anywhere. Little by little, the girls huddled up like sheep. I was out of place and glad to have my marble pouch with me.

The boys were setting up a game of Ringer in the corner of the school yard. There was a full fifteen minutes before the first bell, so I strolled over as if I didn't have a care in the world.

Esau Mooney smiled when he saw me. Daniel was there, too. His hair was longer than long. He had it slicked back with pomade, but it still hung in his eyes as he bent over the ring. He didn't have on a new outfit like the others.

I asked if I could get in the game. As always, there was a big argument about letting me throw lag. Daniel was pretending to count his marbles. He spit in the dirt at my feet, barely missing my shiny shoes. He didn't say a word.

Anthony said, "Oh, let her play, for Pete's sake."

Jacob swaggered around. His jeans were rolled up at the ankles, like James Dean's. "Listen up, men. Let's play Bombsies today."

"Bombsies?" I asked. "What's Bombsies?" My breath caught a bit. Had they learned a new marble game without me?

Anthony explained, "You don't need a cross. And you don't have to knuckle down to shoot. All you need is a pile of marbles. You hold your arm over the ring and let your taw fall on the pile. Whichever marbles you smash, you get to keep."

Jacob laughed. "Don't forget to yell 'Bombs away!'"

"Well, I'm in," I said. It sounded too easy. Suddenly, I was coveting marbles left and right.

"Fine," said Jacob.

I won lag and found out I would be playing against Jacob. He had two pouches of marbles with him. I found out later he'd collected more marbles than God all because of Bombsies. It didn't occur to me to call friendlies and test this new game. How on earth did I even know I had the skills for it?

I didn't, and that was my first mistake. Jacob and Esau had taken a trip to Nebraska, and Jacob had won a steely off his cousin. That's a steel ball bearing. I'd heard of them, but I'd never seen one up close.

"Can I take a look at your new taw?" I asked.

"Sure." Jacob dropped it in my hand. It was heavy in my palm. I examined the steely. I could see my reflection on the surface. I wanted it.

"Give it back," Jacob said, holding out a grimy hand. I handed it over.

Then we voted on whether he'd get to use it or not.

Jacob told me, "A girl's vote doesn't count."

I snuck a glance at the double doors. We didn't want the playground monitor to catch us playing marbles on school grounds.

All of the boys voted yes: Jacob could use the steely. They were really hoping that one of them would win it.

Fat chance. I was going to have it for myself.

Agreeing to play Jacob while he used his steely—that was my second mistake. That blasted steely broke two of my creamies and three of my commies, plus Jacob got my prized blue taw.

I saw it spin the wrong way, and when it bounced out, I yelled, "Quitsies!" But Jacob said I was too late. He scooped it up. As he cradled my beautiful taw in his hand, I gritted my teeth so I wouldn't cry. Things got sort of fuzzy around the edges for me after that. Anger started at my feet and worked its way up my body until I was shaking.

I love that marble. Sometimes I lie back on the grass and put it up to my eye. If I squint and peer through it, I can see all the way to the sun.

Jacob shined it up on his pants as if it had belonged to him all along. When he peered through the taw just like I do, I felt as if my head, or maybe my chest, were going to explode. I reached for the blue taw, but Jacob snatched it away.

I lunged for it. "Give me that back, you cheat!"

Jacob held me at arm's length. "Freedom, I'm not gonna fight you. I won that taw fair and square. Get ahold of yourself."

Daniel said, "This is why you can't play marbles with us anymore. Crybaby."

"Crybaby," Wally Biscotti echoed.

I attacked, pummeling Jacob's stomach with my fists. He blocked me with his arms and laughed. He held my taw above my head, taunting me, so I stomped on his foot. That got him good.

"Darn it, Freedom!" he shouted. "Stop it!"

Wally Biscotti screamed, "Fight, fight, fight!" and the boys surrounded us. A bunch of other kids came over and joined the circle. Templeview Elementary kids always love a good rumble. We were causing an awful scene, but I couldn't help it.

Someone pulled me back. It was Esau. "That's enough. Leave her alone."

He was holding me gently, but I struggled until I was sweaty. "Can't you get my taw back from your brother?"

Esau shook his head. "It won't work."

"Please?"

Jacob put my taw in his pocket and said, "Nope."

"Give it back!" I shouted.

Anthony ran toward the school.

I got loose and ran straight into Daniel. I begged, "Get it back for me, please?"

"I can't. Now stop throwing such a fit." He tried to drag me away, but I kicked at his shin until he let go. "You're nuts," he said.

Miss Spotswood came hurrying over. The boys started shuffling their feet, trying to cover up the ring and the leftover marbles. I'd been beat. "Miss McKenzie, what *are* you doing?" she demanded.

Wasn't it obvious? I realized I was crying and wiped the snot from my face with my arm. My dress was dirty down the front, one knee was bloody, and I'd lost a shoe in the scuffle.

Esau tried to hand me my shoe, but I ignored him and pointed at Jacob. "Gimme my blue taw!"

Jacob stared up at the gathering clouds. "I don't know what you're talking about." His hands were behind his back, probably with his fingers crossed.

The first bell rang. Esau gave my shoe to Miss Spotswood. Everyone was lining up. Daniel, Wally, and Esau abandoned us.

Miss Spotswood looked at the school. She checked her watch. "We'd better settle this inside. Freedom, put on your shoe. And Jacob, please pick up those marbles."

Jacob picked up the rest of the marbles and didn't give a single one back to me. As we walked toward the double doors, I thought about how I was going to explain to Mama that I'd had to clean desks after school. Or worse. I hoped I wouldn't be taking a note home.

"My first graders are waiting for me," Miss Spotswood said. She told Jacob to hurry to his classroom and that she'd deal with him later.

I clenched my fists as he smirked at me and joined a line of sixth graders. I just knew he'd be getting off scot-free. Miss Spotswood led me down the long hall to my new classroom. Nancy's eyes got wide when she saw me. I must have been a sight. I waited while Miss Spotswood whispered to my new teacher, Mrs. Thompson, who was herding my classmates through the door. As they passed, everyone stared at me and my rumpled dress and snotty face.

"Try to have a better day, Freedom," Miss Spotswood said as she walked away.

My pretty new teacher looked at me. She had soft brown eyes and smelled like peppermint. "Freedom, I'm sorry we have to meet under these circumstances. I assume you know that boys and girls should not be roughhousing. Fighting is against school rules."

"We weren't roughhousing. He stole something from me." My nose was still dripping, but I didn't have a handkerchief.

"It doesn't matter. You should find a teacher if you have trouble in the school yard."

How could a teacher get my taw back when I wasn't supposed to be playing marbles in the first place?

My face grew hotter as I stood in front of her desk with my back to my new class. Mrs. Thompson wrote out a letter on crisp white paper. She even had pretty penmanship, but I couldn't make out the swirly words.

"I hope we aren't starting off on the wrong foot, Freedom." She folded the note up twice and took a long hatpin from her drawer and used it to pin the note to my dress. "Furthermore—and I'm sure you already know this— marbles are a boys' game."

I sighed.

"You may excuse yourself to use the girls' room. Please wash your face. And find a handkerchief. It's time to start our day." I hung my head while twenty-six pairs of eyes followed me out of the room.

I washed my tear-stained face and cleaned up my bloody knee in the bathroom, and I thought about all the ways I could get rid of the note before I got home. But I knew I'd chicken out. Last year, after I cut off the end of one of Judy Bernard's pigtails, I'd buried a note in the kitchen trash. Mama found it, and that got me in more trouble than ever.

I spent the entire first day of fifth grade with a blasted note pinned to my dress.

When I got home, I hid it in my pocket. I waited until after supper to give the note to Mama. Higgie was already in bed, and Daddy was listening to the radio out on the back porch. She was sitting at the kitchen table reading *The Common Sense Book of Baby and Child Care*.

As I held out the note, dread filled my very soul. "Mama, my new teacher sent this home with me today."

I paced around while she read the note and then tucked it in her bra. "Freedom Jane," she said, "you are trying to fit in where you don't belong. Girls your age do not play games with boys."

"But, Mama—" I stopped. There was no use explaining.

"No buts. You are finished with marbles. Go and get them, please."

I went into my room and lingered there. When I came back to the kitchen, I was clutching the pouch for dear life. I had to think of something. After the church fiasco, Daddy hadn't found the chance to ask Mama about the competition.

"Mama, I won't bring them to school ever again. I promise."

She said, "When I was your age, I knew when to give up. You haven't learned yet."

I should've hidden my marbles when I got home from school. I should've torn up the note for sure. Mostly, I wished I could've punched Jacob Mooney in the eye when I had the chance.

Mama held out her hand. "Freedom, give the bag of marbles to me."

I stared my mother square in the eyes. She meant business. Of course, she always means business. I laid my pouch on the kitchen table and ran from the room.

Mama called after me, "You'll see. I'm doing this for your own good."

I cried and cried that night, but I knew Mama wouldn't budge. Even Daddy couldn't get her to change her mind. And my beautiful blue taw was gone forever.

I wasn't sure who I was madder at: my mama, Jacob Mooney, or myself.

Chapter Eleven
Breaking Pearls

SEPTEMBER 16, 1959

Today, after school, I trudged home with my books and my lunch pail. I had a headache behind my eyes. When I came through the back door, Mama said, "Why the long face?"

She had the ironing board set up in the kitchen. A straw basket full of clothes sat on the floor by her feet. The dark curls on her neck were wet with perspiration.

"Nothing," I told her. I set my things on the counter and rummaged around in the Frigidaire for a snack.

The steamy smell of starch and Borax hung in the air. As Mama spit on the hot iron, it hissed. She shook a shirt from the basket and laid it out on top of the ironing board. Higgie was at the table, pressing his Silly Putty onto the funny pages of the newspaper.

"Look, Freedom, it's Snoopy." He showed me the Silly Putty. I ignored him.

Did I dare tell Mama that fifth grade is hard, especially when your only friend sits all the way across the room? I poured a tall glass of milk and sat at the table.

Mama said, "Out with it."

Once I started talking, it came out in a rush. "Nancy and I were whispering while Mrs. Thompson was writing on the board, so I got moved to the back-row corner, and Nancy got moved to the front-row corner. Now I'll barely even see her all day. We don't get to talk until recess, and recess is boring."

"You shouldn't be talking while the teacher is teaching," Mama scolded. "Are you doing well in arithmetic?"

I told Mama that arithmetic is my favorite subject. And it is. It's the most fun when Mrs. Thompson writes a complicated division problem on the board. She'll call out five names. We'll all stand up. When she says "Go," we race to the board and use long sticks of chalk to work out the problems. And whoever solves the problem first gets a lemon drop from the jar on her desk. I win every time.

We used to play jacks or hopscotch at recess. Now all of the girls stand together by the double doors, flipping their hair, trying to get the attention of the older boys. Some of the girls wear lipstick. Nancy says it doesn't matter. Come spring, the two of us are going to skate around the neighborhood in our new roller skates. We'll put pink pompoms on the laces and pretend we're Roller Derby girls.

Daniel and the boys have started playing football at recess. No one ever has any marbles with them anymore. I don't know if they still play Ringer at the park. It makes me wonder who I'd be playing against when the marble competition finally rolls around. Daniel acts as if he doesn't walk two feet behind me all the way to school and back every single day.

I told Mama, "I swear, Mrs. Thompson hasn't quite forgiven me for fighting with Jacob over my taw on the first day of school."

She took another shirt from the basket. "Well, that's your own fault."

I opened my mouth to argue. But instead I said, "Sally Jensen wore pants to school on the second day, and now the other girls sometimes wear pants, too. Nancy says it's because Sally is the most popular girl in school."

Mama said, "Young ladies should wear dresses to school."

"I know, Mama. I'm not saying I want to wear pants or anything. I'm saying—"

The washing machine began making a terrible racket on the spin cycle. That means Mama was washing rugs again.

"It's just . . . things are so different. I miss Daniel."

"I'm sure you do, dear. Can't you and Nancy make other friends?"

I looked at Mama and said, "I really miss shooting marbles."

She turned over the shirt to press the collar and moved

the iron back and forth. "It's only been a week. There's more to life than marbles, Freedom."

I knew that. But there was no way I could talk to Mama about how Betty Branson's acting like a fool in love with Esau Mooney. How she puts on her mother's bright pink lipstick after lunch and spends all her recess time following him around, asking if she can hold his coat while he plays football. Secretly, it makes my skin prickle when Esau smiles at Betty.

And whenever he says "Hello, Freedom," I get tongue-tied.

Still, I would never follow a boy around just to hold his dumb old coat. And I'd never want to be like Linda Pratt, who got caught holding Daniel's hand behind the school.

Mama said, "The only thing you have to worry about is your report card. Daniel's growing up, and it's time you grew up, too. You'd do well to remember that."

She hung the pressed shirt on a hanger and stretched her back. Her baby belly was poking out in the tent of a dress she was wearing.

Higgie started to cry. Mama said, "You've got that Silly Putty all over your pants, Higginbotham!" She hustled him to the bathroom for some soap and water.

I drank the rest of my milk and said to the empty kitchen, "I think I want to lie down."

I went straight to my room. The moment I hit the pillow, I closed my eyes.

A little while later Mama woke me, calling out, "I have

to drop off a dessert at the church, Freedom. Do you think you could stay here alone for a half hour or so and watch Higgie until Daddy gets home from work?"

I sat up. Mama trusted me enough to watch Higgie!

I found Mama at her vanity table. "I'll give you a nickel for babysitting," she said.

"Okay."

She saw my tired face. "I'm sorry you had a tough day." She pulled me close. She's been doing that a lot lately. I kind of like this new side of Mama, so I hugged her back. She grabbed her hairbrush. "Freedom Jane, how in heaven's name did you get this rat's nest on the back of your head?"

I shrugged. My head jerked with every stroke of her brush. "I was having a nap."

She grumbled, "I don't know why you can't sit nicely and do your cross-stich, or finish that paint-by-numbers kit you got for your birthday."

I can never please her. If I embroider on hankies, she criticizes my stitches. Too tight, too far apart, too loose. If the stitches are perfect, she'll say something about my dirty fingernails.

Mama dipped into the hair bow box and pulled out two rubber bands. She put the bands in her mouth while she drew a part in my hair with her comb. Before I knew it, she'd made two perfect pigtails and tied a red ribbon around each of them.

"There," she said. "Don't you look nice." My hair felt

too tight. But I didn't tell her that or that I was getting too old for pigtails.

"Thank you, Mama."

"I have to hurry now," she said.

I flopped down on the faded rug to watch while she put on her face. First, she drew on her eyebrows with a special pencil. The lipstick came next. When she was done, she blotted her face and neck with her fluffy pink powder puff. The fine powder floated around and settled on her dresser. Mama's room always smells good.

She spit on the mascara pan and pulled the brush around and around until the black glob was ready to put on her eyes. She pinched the thin brush between her fingers and opened her eyes wide. "Someday, Freedom," she said, "I'll be teaching you how to put on *your* face." Mama brushed the mascara onto her lashes. Then she held her face still—not blinking—so the mascara wouldn't smear. Her hair was piled up in a beehive, and she kept fussing over it. It was awful big, if you ask me. She kept pushing it down in spots, but it bounced right back.

She attempted to wiggle into her best girdle, and I couldn't help but smile at her funny dance. She saw me watching and grinned. "Guess I'm getting too big for a girdle." She peeled the girdle off and said I could play for a few minutes while she went to the bathroom one more time. "But don't you wrinkle up my dress."

Mama hardly ever leaves me alone in her and Daddy's

room. I carefully avoided the green dress that was laid out on her white chenille bedspread. Even Higgie knows that we aren't allowed on Mama and Daddy's bed.

I examined the vials and pots and spray cans on top of the vanity. The mascara pan was still wet from Mama's spit. I took the cap off the Strawberry Cream lipstick and smelled it. It didn't smell like strawberries, but I put a layer on my lips and mashed them together anyway.

Mama had a copy of *Life* magazine on her nightstand. Mrs. Jackie Kennedy smiled from the cover. She was wearing pearls and a lovely pink sweater, and was sitting pretty with her husband. Wouldn't you know her pink lipstick matched her outfit perfectly? I hope I'm half as ladylike as she is when I grow up. Mr. Kennedy smiled like he had a secret. I don't care if Mrs. Kennedy's a Catholic and a Democrat to boot, she's prettier than Marilyn Monroe any day of the week. Mama says Miss Monroe is trashy, and I'm not supposed to talk about her.

I stared in the mirror and pretended I was a movie star.

Mama had left her jewelry on the table. I tried on her thin wedding band. I clipped some sparkly earrings to my earlobes, and even though they pinched something awful, I kept them on for a whole minute.

Bored with the stuff on Mama's vanity, I snooped in the dresser drawers. In the bottom one I found a bundle of love letters from Daddy tied up neatly with pink ribbon. Under that was a framed picture of Mama's daddy. Something about his eyes made me put him back facedown. In the middle drawer I found a bunch of filled-in crossword puzzles from the newspaper, along with magazine clippings about beauty and fashion tips, some embroidered hankies, and a broken watch.

I spied a shiny black box nestled under a yellow silk nightgown. I took out the box and opened it. The hinges creaked. I held my breath. If Mama found me snooping through her private things, she'd ground me for sure.

The bathroom door was still shut tight. I peeked into the box. You know what was inside? Mama's wedding day pearls! I was coveting them. I couldn't help it. They were so pretty. I picked them up. They were cold and smooth, and the clasp looked like real gold. I licked one. It tasted of Mama's hair spray. I wiped my tongue on the edge of my blouse.

"Mama," I yelled, "can I try on your wedding day pearls?"

"No!" she yelled back.

I put the pearls in the drawer and picked up *Life* again.

I tried to read, but I was itching to put on the wedding day pearls. Mostly because Mrs. Jackie Kennedy was smiling at me from the cover of that blasted magazine as if she were telling me it was okay.

I took out the black satin box again. I would put on the pearls. Just to see how they looked on my neck. After that I would take care of Higgie like a grown-up girl. Maybe take him over to see Mrs. Zierk. Mama would never know if I put the pearls right back after.

Well, tiny mice must have been chewing on the string, because as I was turning and admiring myself in the mirror, the whole strand slid from my neck as fast as a waterfall. The pearls rolled all over the hardwood floor and under the bed and dresser before I could stop them.

Mama came out, screeching like a rooster. She grabbed my arm. "Those were my mama's! The best jewelry I have! Wait till your daddy gets home!"

I felt so sad when she said that. I'm not afraid of my daddy. He wouldn't hurt a flea. Even when I'm bad, he'll smile and pat the top of my head. She let go of my arm and just sat on the bed, staring at the floor. I was sad that I had hurt Mama's feelings.

I spent the rest of the afternoon in my room all by myself. Mrs. Nelsen from down the street came and sat in the living room with Higgie.

The Chevy pulled up in the driveway right before supper. Daddy was late. I listened for his voice. I didn't think he'd come in and punish me, but you never know. I stood in the shadow of my doorway so I could hear their conversation.

When Mama told him what I'd done, Daddy didn't say anything except "Willie, you've been meaning to get those pearls restrung. Now you can do it and wear them more often."

I scrambled back into my room as I heard Daddy coming down the hall. He knocked on the door and told me to come out and eat supper. When I came out to the kitchen,

Mama's eyes were all red, but she gave me a hug and told me she wasn't mad anymore.

"I'm sorry, Mama," I said.

"You'll still have to miss *The Lawrence Welk Show* after supper." She knows I love to watch the dancers and the floating bubbles.

We ate in near silence. Daddy had three beers and acted like he'd had some others before he'd come home.

The meat loaf was dry and my baked potato was tough, but I told Mama it all tasted good. After I helped with the dishes, Daddy said I had to go to bed before Higgie.

I knew it was for the best.

Daddy came to tuck me in. "With the new baby coming and all, can't you try harder to get along with your mama?" he asked.

"I'll try, Daddy," I said. And I meant it.

He kissed me good night. His breath smelled like beer. "I know you will, Sugar Beet."

Chapter Twelve
Spitting Rocks

OCTOBER 3, 1959

On Saturday morning I walked to the beauty salon with Mama. Higgie stayed at home with Mrs. Nelsen. I brought *The Witch of Blackbird Pond*. I had to write a book report about it by Monday.

Mrs. Clark, the owner of the salon, had on a blue smock, and her hair was dyed so light it was practically pink. "My, my, Mrs. McKenzie, you sure are getting ready to have that baby! When are you due?"

Mama smiled weakly. "About two more months."

She got comfortable, and Mrs. Clark pumped her foot on the bar under the chair until Mama was high enough for Mrs. Clark's liking. She whipped a black cape up in the air, and the two of them began gossiping the minute the cape was tied around Mama's neck. I sat in an extra chair and tried to read my book.

While Mama got a shampoo, they gossiped about movie stars, especially Elizabeth Taylor and how she stole her friend Debbie Reynolds's husband, Eddie Fisher. They talked about the best place to get ground beef. And what toilet paper costs these days.

As Mrs. Clark rolled sections of Mama's wet hair in metal curlers, she said, "I wonder if Mrs. Kroger knows about Mrs. Coyle and you-know-who?"

Mama said, "Little pitchers have big ears"—whatever that means—and they changed the subject.

After Mama got all settled in under the jumbo hair dryer with a magazine, Mrs. Clark turned her attention to me. "Freedom, how would you like to look more sophisticated?" she asked. Now, wasn't that the pot calling the kettle black? I realized her pink hair was really a wig when she stuck her comb underneath for a good scratch. Her perfume smelled like bug spray. She also snapped her gum, which I know Mama can't stand.

"I don't really think about stuff like that," I said.

Mrs. Clark poked Mama's elbow with her comb and shouted over the dryer, "Willie, why don't we give Freedom a permanent wave?" Mrs. Clark flipped through one of her hairdo magazines and showed me a picture of the perky Mouseketeer from TV, Annette Funicello. "Like it?"

I couldn't picture that hairstyle on me. Mama tipped up

the dryer head. "What do you think, Freedom? You *do* have a date with your daddy tonight."

Daddy and I were going to see *Sleeping Beauty* at the drive-in movie theater right at sunset. I thought it would be nice to look pretty for him.

At the drive-in, the attendant comes by and hangs a speaker on your car window so you can hear the movie. You can sit on the hood if you want. Waitresses in white uniforms bring cheeseburgers and fries and sodas and boxes of candy on trays that attach to the window. We'd agreed we were going to have popcorn and Junior Mints. I had bragged to everyone at school about it all week. I've been only once before.

"You would look more mature with shorter hair," Mrs. Clark said.

I wasn't convinced. But I didn't know how to say so. Before I knew it, I was wearing a cape like Mama's.

For the next half hour, Mrs. Clark snipped at my hair and rolled it into tiny pink plastic curlers. I had to sit forever under that hot cape with a mixture of smelly solution on my head. My eyes burned, and my neck got terribly itchy.

Mrs. Clark told me to sit still about a million times. Easy for her to say. Her hair didn't smell as bad as mine. Mrs. Clark took out Mama's curlers. She used a thin comb and a can of hair spray until she set Mama's hair in the perfect beehive.

It was almost lunchtime. My stomach was growling. I was sure the permanent solution was burning a permanent hole in my scalp. I closed my eyes, tired of holding my head up.

After what seemed like another hour, the timer went *ding*, and I got to lean back in the shampoo chair while Mrs. Clark rinsed out my hair under the warm spray. After she dried the whole mess with a towel, I sat under the big dryer, too. When my hair was nearly dry, Mrs. Clark took out the curlers and teased and back-combed and sprayed me with the hair spray until I could taste it. She pushed on my head here and there and patted it down in the back.

When she was done fussing, Mrs. Clark twirled my chair around so I could see myself in the mirror. "*Ta-da!*"

My hair was as short and curly as a dumb old poodle's.

Mama clapped her hands. "I love it! Wasn't that fun, Freedom?"

She paid Mrs. Clark, and I pouted all the way home.

The first thing Higgie said to me was "Pee-u, you stink." Then he turned to Mama. "When will Daddy be home?"

"Not until tonight. You two, go and play. I need to rest awhile."

I wanted to go and show my hairdo to Mrs. Zierk. Mama had decided that free piano lessons were a mighty fine deal, so I've been visiting with our neighbor after school, even though I'm not playing much piano.

The thing is, Mrs. Zierk has almost as many rules as Mama, like I have to take my shoes off at the door. And I have to wash my hands before I do anything. I don't really mind. She always has something special for us to do together. I'm learning how to knit. I'm making Mama a Christmas present. It's a red-and-white striped afghan. Mrs. Zierk makes me sit in her hard rocking chair while I'm knitting, and if I miss a stitch, she rips out the entire row instead of letting me pick up the stitch the next time around. I have to do four rows every day I'm there. The blanket is scratchy, but I think Mama is going to love it. Red is her favorite color.

I brought Higgie to Mrs. Zierk's. She looked him up and down and said, "I sure don't enjoy children who misbehave."

Higgie saluted. "Yes, ma'am."

He was good for about ten minutes. He played on the floor with a handful of wooden beads and a piece of yarn, making himself a necklace. Then he got bored. When Mrs. Zierk wasn't looking, he took one of the precious teacups she keeps on a shelf in the dining room. Higgie had it up in the air, dangling from his pinky finger. Sure enough, the delicate handle broke clean off. There was no way to hide it.

Mrs. Zierk sent Higgie home. She told him, "Don't come back unless you can behave next time."

I like having Mrs. Zierk all to myself. She's crocheting a whole layette with yellow, white, and light green yarn for our new baby, including tiny booties and matching caps. It's going to be a surprise for Mama.

We worked on our projects together as the radio blared in the background. She likes listening to old-time programs, like Ma Perkins and Young Doctor Malone, and classical piano music. It's good to have someone to talk with—it's also good to have someone to be quiet with. Especially someone who knows all about my troubles.

Mrs. Zierk told me my hair was too short. "But it will grow," she said. "How is your mama feeling?"

I told Mrs. Zierk that I didn't see how Mama's belly could get any bigger.

She chuckled.

I did my four rows of knitting, and afterward, we sat at the piano together. I've decided that piano is not for me. I'd rather listen to Mrs. Zierk play. Her favorite composer is named Rachmaninoff. When her fingers fly over the keys during a piece called "Flight of the Bumblebee," it's the only time I ever see her with a genuine smile that goes from ear to ear.

Mama was folding laundry at the kitchen table as I came in the back door. Higgie was having a snack on his stool. Soon it would be time for the movie!

"Hi, Mama!"

"You getting excited?" She grinned.

"I sure am."

"Well, get ready. I've laid out a clean dress for you." I went to my room and put on my nice navy-blue dress.

I decided to sit on the couch quietly and wait for Daddy. I wouldn't get dirty no matter what. Higgie took his train out. He lay on the floor, saying "*Choo, choo*" over and over again. I put my fingers in my ears and wondered what

Daddy was going to think about my hair.

The telephone rang. Mama answered and started yelling. I knew better than to go into the kitchen. But I sneaked over and peeked in the door. It was half past seven.

Mama was standing at the sink, rubbing her pregnant belly and shouting into the phone, "Just tell me: was Homer at Mike's Pub or wasn't he?"

She hung up and called me into the kitchen. I shuffled in slowly. Mama wouldn't look at me as she said, "Your daddy wrapped the Chevy around a tree."

We stood together for a minute, and I pressed my arm against her hard, warm belly. The baby inside kicked. Mama didn't even notice. The way she had said "your daddy" hurt my ears. She sat down at the table.

"What do you mean, Mama?"

"He wrecked the car, Freedom." She seemed awful tired all of a sudden. She wiped her eyes with the corner of her apron. "Uncle Mort says that your daddy fell asleep at the wheel on their way home from the shop. He needs a couple of stitches in his head." She must've seen how worried I was because her voice softened. "He'll be home soon."

I began to cry. It was getting dark outside. The movie would be starting without me. Mama patted my shoulder. Higgie came in and crawled onto Mama's lap. I would've given anything for her to sweep me onto her lap, too. But she didn't. She put Higgie down and swept up her purse instead.

"Go on and watch the television, and let me think."

I watched *The Dick Clark Show* with Higgie. He didn't ask what was going on. Mama banged things around in the kitchen. It smelled like the casserole had dried up in the pan. She talked to Aunt Janie on the phone twice. Finally, I saw headlights flash across the wall of the living room. I ran to the front window. Mama came in and said, "Get away from there, Freedom Jane!"

Higgie called, "Daddy, Daddy!"

But it was only Uncle Mort at the door. His skin looked gray under the porch light. A blood-soaked bandage was stuck to his forehead, and he had some paperwork in his hands.

I waited for Daddy, but he didn't appear. Mama asked, "Where is he?"

Uncle Mort whispered, "Jail."

Mama gasped. Then she pressed her lips together. I knew Daddy was in big trouble. I waited to see what Mama would say next. She stared at the carpet and asked Uncle Mort, "Are you hungry? Let's get something in your stomach."

Uncle Mort's eyes were real shiny, and I smelled beer when he passed by. In the kitchen, Higgie climbed up on his knee. Every now and then, Uncle Mort gave him a bounce. I just stood there, waiting for someone to tell me something.

"It was the darndest thing," Uncle Mort said. "The car had a mind of its own."

Mama tied on an apron and fluttered awkwardly around the kitchen like a butterfly with one wing. She handed Uncle Mort a glass of water. I was confused. I couldn't figure out why she wasn't yelling again. As she went to put on the coffee, I couldn't stand it anymore.

"Who's taking me to the movies?" I shouted. "That's what I want to know!"

Mama shushed me. Uncle Mort shook his head. "You can't go tonight," he said.

"But Daddy *promised*."

"I'm sorry," Uncle Mort said. "He'll have to take you another time. What a shame, too. It looks like you had your hair done special."

Mama put a plate of burnt casserole in front of Uncle Mort. She slapped another plate down for Higgie and said, "Have some, Freedom."

She put a plate in front of me before I could respond. I couldn't stop staring at Uncle Mort. He was shoveling food into his mouth. It felt like I'd never seen him before in my life.

Uncle Mort stopped eating. "What's the matter?"

I crossed my arms. I was so mad I could spit rocks. "It was the last night to see *Sleeping Beauty* at the drive-in. And you've ruined it." I stomped my foot. "I never get to do anything I want to do!"

"Freedom Jane McKenzie!" Mama said. "Apologize right now!"

"I won't. He's drunk. I smell it. He and Daddy are two peas in a pod. I've heard you say it!"

"I did not!" Mama said.

"It's true!" I ran to my room and threw myself on my bed. I heard Uncle Mort leave. I lay there with tears streaming down my face.

How was I supposed to tell everyone at school about *Sleeping Beauty* when I'd missed the whole thing?

Later, Mama came in to put Higgie to bed. He got all settled in and whispered to me, "What's wrong, Freedom?"

"None of your business," I mumbled.

Mama sat on the edge of my bed. I kept my eyes closed. She stroked my cheek. "I'm sorry about your daddy. He doesn't mean to mess things up."

"But he's in jail because he messed up awful big tonight. Right?"

Mama sat very still. She cradled her belly. "Yes. And I hope he'll learn a lesson this time."

I wasn't sure that he would, but I couldn't help wondering, "Do you think he had anything to eat? Do you think he's cold?"

She whispered, "I'm sure Daddy's asleep by now." Mama rose and smoothed out my covers. The tiredness in her eyes told me to stop asking questions. The floor creaked under her as she crept out of my room. She stopped in the doorway. "Everything's going to look better in the morning. You'll see."

That's just it. I couldn't see how things would be okay at all. My daddy used to say that he loved me more than anything. But, at that moment, I knew he couldn't possibly love me more than beer. And that's the truth. There was one more question I had to ask. I took a deep breath and whispered, "Mama?"

The hall light made a halo around Mama's hair. "Yes, Freedom?"

"Is Daddy a drunk?"

Mama's lips barely moved when she whispered, "Yes."

Chapter Thirteen

Swallowing Marbles

OCTOBER 16, 1959

It's no secret around town how Daddy wrecked the Chevy. He keeps saying he's going to join the alcoholic's group that meets at the Catholic church on the edge of town, but I haven't seen him do it yet. He's still drinking a beer—or three—with his supper. And he is still bowling on Tuesdays with Uncle Mort, coming in later than ever.

He had to see a judge about all the trouble he got in and pay for his fines. He was issued a ticket for reckless driving and also got a talking-to at work. He'd gone over to the Wilsons' on Canal Avenue for a house call, and Mrs. Wilson wouldn't let Daddy in. She said she didn't want a criminal working on her television picture tube and to send someone else.

Mama told Aunt Janie that some people need to mind

their own business. She doesn't want anyone else to talk badly about our family. Just her. She's been calling Daddy a "jailbird."

The morning he got out of jail, he brought home a single red rose for Mama. She said, "If you think a flower is going to make up for last night, you've got another think coming."

She put it in water, though. "Your little girl's heart is broken over that movie she missed." Mama pointed to me.

When Daddy saw my poodle hair, he said, "Oh, Willie. What'd you go and cut her hair off for?"

Mama told him I'd asked for the permanent. I didn't argue with her. I didn't feel like talking.

Daddy pulled a caboose from his pocket for Higgie's train set. And I got another dumb Barbie doll. This one has brown hair, and she's wearing the exact same zebra-striped bathing suit as my other Barbie. I had to say thank you. But I barely whispered it, so I didn't mean it.

All Mama said was "Freedom, you're in quite a mood."

I *was* in a mood. A *permanent* mood. Daddy didn't even mention the movie.

This week we got a new old car. The Chevy got towed to the junkyard because it couldn't be fixed. Daddy bought a DeSoto. It's puke green, and inside it smells of rotten knockwurst and cigarette butts. Every time Daddy turns off the engine, the new old car rumbles and shakes like a dragon. I'm waiting for the neighbors to complain to Mama. That would serve Daddy right. Higgie loves the backseat because it's big enough for both of us to lie down side by side. I'll never like that car.

I miss the Chevy.

We bought the DeSoto from the used car man two towns over because Daddy didn't trust Nancy's father to sell him a good car. Nancy's been out of school for two days since her mother's been in the hospital with pneumonia. She's been staying at her daddy's apartment. And I'm not allowed to play over there. I'm glad, because her daddy gives me the shivers.

At school, the kids have been talking about how wild Homer McKenzie is. I can't stand it. I've been eating my lunch alone. Even an A– on my arithmetic test didn't make me feel any better about things.

It was too cold to play outside tonight, so Higgie and I were watching this new cowboy show *Bonanza* on the color television that Daddy brought home. He traded the lawn mower for it with some man who'd bought a bigger television for his wife. I don't know what Daddy is going to do next summer without a lawn mower.

"We'll get a goat," Daddy said. Mama rolled her eyes.

Secretly, Mama is pleased. The new television has a record player in the same cabinet. She shined the cabinet with furniture polish and put a white doily on top to hide the scratches. She's been dusting it twice a day. We must be the last ones on the street to get a color TV—except for Daniel and Mrs. Zierk.

Daddy was out, so I was supposed to keep an eye on

Higgie while Mama baked a lemon meringue pie.

No, she didn't want my help, thank you. And I wasn't to run through the kitchen, either, or else the meringue would fall.

Higgie lay on the floor, chewing on the end of his crummy old blanket, eyes glued to the screen. Every once in a while, he stuck a finger in his nose and left it there. I had already colored with him in his ratty old coloring book. I rocked in the fuzzy green rocker. We got it with some of Grandma McKenzie's things when she passed.

That chair is the best invention in the world, next to the color television. Sometimes I'll spin Higgie around and around. I stop when his eyes get crossed. He'll say he's going to throw up, and I know it's my turn. The chair is ugly as all get-out, but when you're in it, you don't notice that.

I pressed the round green buttons on the fabric and pretended to be the first woman astronaut rocketing through space. I counted down to liftoff: "Five, four, three, two, one . . ."

Every time I leaned back for takeoff, the springs under my bottom went *brrriing!*

I spied one of my cat's-eye marbles, lost under the couch. So much had been going on, I hadn't dared to ask Mama about getting my pouch back. I jumped from the chair and grabbed it. I scrambled up before Higgie could steal my seat from me. But his eyes never left the program. Higgie gets that way around a television set.

If only I had *two* marbles. It would only take two to practice for the competition.

Mama stuck her head into the living room just then, and I don't know why, but I popped the cat's-eye into my mouth and pretended I was scratching my stomach.

Mama said, "Stop rocking so hard on that chair. You're going to break it."

I should've spit the marble out the minute Mama went back into the kitchen, but instead I moved the cat's-eye around in my mouth with my tongue. It was cold and smooth like Mama's pearls. It didn't taste very good, either, but it still felt good in my mouth.

If Mama knew I had a marble, would she take it from me? Could I use my single marble to play with the boys and win a whole bunch? Maybe Daniel would let me borrow some of his marbles. I thought about asking Esau for some. Whenever he's nearby, I can feel his eyes on me.

I sat back and rocked, rolling that marble around with my tongue as I watched the TV. I got caught up in the show and laughed.

I must have laughed too hard, because I sucked that cat's-eye right into my windpipe. My eyes went wide when I realized I couldn't breathe. Just when I thought I was going to choke to death, I swallowed it.

Afterward, I sat real still. I blinked a couple of times and swallowed again. The cat's-eye was gone. It was probably already on its way to my belly. I got hot all over. I wasn't sure whether to tell Mama or not. Chances were good that I'd be in big trouble if I told her. But what would happen to the marble if I didn't tell her?

I might die.

For sure I'd have *no* marbles, again.

I remembered the time Higgie stuck a pebble in his ear. He had to be put to sleep at the hospital before the doctor pulled it out with tiny tweezers. He didn't get into trouble at all. Mama told everyone that her bitty baby was lucky he wasn't deaf. And she hugged him over and over when he woke up in the hospital. He even got ice cream.

I decided I'd better tell her.

When I went into the kitchen, she was taking the pie from the oven. The meringue was high with perfectly golden brown peaks. It looked like a picture in a magazine. I waited until she set it on top of the stove before I said, "Mama?"

"Don't move," she told me.

I froze. The meringue stayed high.

"What is it, Freedom?"

"Mama . . . I've swallowed a marble."

She hollered a swear word that I'd never heard and dropped her oven mitts. She picked up the telephone and called Mike's Pub, tapping her foot while she waited for Daddy to come to the phone.

When he did, she yelled into the receiver, "Come home!"

You know what she did next? Mama sat down at the table and had a good cry. She sobbed into a dish towel while I stood there. She went on and on. I didn't know what else to do, so I went back to the living room and waited.

By the time Daddy got home, Mama had me wrapped up in a blanket, tight as a mummy. I couldn't have held her hand if I'd wanted to. Daddy picked up Higgie and put him in the front of the DeSoto while Mama and I sat in the back.

We've never driven so fast.

It turned out they couldn't do much for me at the hospital. I had to take two big old spoonfuls of castor oil. And I didn't get to drink a Dr Pepper afterward to cut the oily taste. Then Doc Brooks sent us back home to "see if it shows up." He told Mama to watch my stool for it. I don't know how watching the step stool in the kitchen is going to help.

Aunt Janie and Uncle Mort came over. Aunt Janie brought a tuna casserole. Nobody was talking much. Uncle Mort paced around the living room.

Daddy tucked me into bed with a hot-water bottle for my tummy. He pulled the covers up around me. "Your mama's gone to bed."

I felt bad for making her worry. Mama's already been upset about the bills from Daddy's accident. They all ate a quiet supper without me. I didn't even get a piece of Mama's perfect pie.

Mama had talked all the way home about why I had a marble in my mouth in the first place. That's one of those hard questions that grown-ups ask. I still don't know the right answer.

She said, "I *was* thinking about letting you play in that silly marble competition, but I've decided that you are *never* going to see a marble again."

I know my marble pouch is probably in the top drawer of Mama's dresser. That's where she keeps everything that she takes from Higgie.

Someday soon I'll get it back. And when I do, I'm going to win my beautiful blue taw from Jacob Meanie. And become the Marble Queen of Idaho Falls.

No matter what Mama says.

Chapter Fourteen

Winner Takes All

OCTOBER 22, 1959

Doc Brooks was right. The cat's-eye showed up, three days later. Let's just say, it's better off in the trash now.

While Mama was making awful lumpy oatmeal for breakfast, I made a decision. I had only three weeks to get ready for the marble competition. And I couldn't do it without my marbles.

Before I knew it, I'd sneaked into Mama's room and grabbed my pouch out of her drawer. I guess I was "bound and determined," like Mama always says.

I promised myself as soon as I was done with them I'd put the marbles right back. I needed to practice shooting, and the only way to do it was to push my way into a game after school—if the boys were even playing anymore.

Fifth grade really is a whole lot harder than fourth.

Just when I think things are all right between me and Mrs. Thompson, some kind of trouble comes up. Last week she thought I wasn't keeping my eyes on my own spelling test. She made me stand at the blackboard for fifteen minutes with my nose in the circle she'd drawn.

And today the whole class got into trouble because of our lousy vocabulary lesson. Nobody could spell the words she'd assigned this week. All twenty-seven of us had to stay after school and write the list of ten words over again. Who needs to know how to spell *splendor*, anyhow?

On the way out I said to Nancy, "I'm going to try to get into a marble game at the park. Want to come?"

She shook her head. "I wish I could. My mother is finally feeling better, but she still needs my help at home."

It was quarter to four by the time I made it over to Highland Park. I figured I wouldn't be fibbing if I told Mama I had to stay after school.

The wind was strong, and the leaves were twirling around on the sidewalk under my feet. I shivered in my thin jacket, wondering if I should've worn the woolly long underwear that Mama had laid out on the bed for me in the morning. But long underwear always rolls down, and it itches like crazy. It was back home, shoved under my pillow.

The boys were there milling around, and I could tell by all the pushing and name-calling that whatever game they'd just finished hadn't gone well.

When Jacob saw me, he said, "Look, it's Poodle Girl."

I patted my hair. It was getting longer, but it was still pretty poufy.

Daniel wasn't wearing a coat. He wouldn't look at me. I thought about all the times he'd sat in my kitchen eating Mama's cooking. Didn't he miss me at all?

I looked at Esau, who was smiling.

"Anyone want to play some Ringer?" I asked.

Wally Biscotti said, "You can't play!" He was wearing a coat that was two sizes too big. You could barely see his hands.

I put my hands on my hips just like Mama does. "And why not?"

"The new rule is that girls can't play. Ever again." He spit into the dirt.

I stuck my chin in the air. "Well, I started the marble season with you boys, and I aim to finish it. Who wants to throw lag?"

Daniel looked up. "Nope. You can't play."

"Besides, we're already done for the day," said Wally.

"Come on. Please?" I knew I sounded whiny.

"Why don't we put it to a vote?" Esau suggested.

The boys huddled together, whispering and chuckling until I was ready to scream.

Finally, Esau said, "Sorry, Freedom. It was four to one. Besides, everyone is pretty much out of good marbles. They're all chipped up from playing Bombsies. Except for some of mine. And I'm saving those for the Autumn Jubilee."

Anthony was jumping up and down, trying to stay warm. "I'm ready to go home."

"Who cares about marbles anyway?" said Daniel. "I'm done with them. I got a football for my birthday. A real leather one. Let's go over to my yard and play catch."

Wally Biscotti's fat cheeks were bright red from the wind. "Naw, it's too cold."

"You have to play with me," I argued. "I want to win my taw back."

Daniel glared at me. "Maybe you shouldn't have played keepsies with it last time."

"Here." Esau stepped forward. He rummaged through his marble sack and took out my blue taw. "I won it off Jacob." He dropped it into my hand.

I peered into my taw. Not a scratch on it. It was still perfectly blue and sparkly inside. Still mine. I was so happy I kissed it. "Thank you, Esau."

He shrugged. "I guess I'll be playing against you at the competition?" He rubbed at the back of his neck like he does during a tense game.

Jacob pushed his face near mine. "Ha! She won't be there. Girls can't even enter!"

I yelled right back at him, "The announcement in the paper didn't say anything about that!"

Esau said, "Well, I guess we'll know soon enough."

Jacob grabbed his brother. "Are you done talking to this poodle girl? Let's go already. I'm freezing."

Esau looked right into my eyes. "See you around, Freedom."

His brother punched him on the arm and said, "You're it." And they raced from the park. Wally ran after them.

Anthony trailed along behind. "Wait for me, fellas."

Daniel kicked at the dirt. "I've got to go, too. I'll bet my dinner's almost ready." He shivered a bit. I knew darn well his mom wouldn't be home until after six, but I didn't challenge him on it. "See ya," he said.

I watched him walk away, his back hunched.

"Daniel?"

He turned around. "What?"

"You want to come over for supper? I'm sure Mama won't mind. And the kitchen will be nice and warm until your mama gets off work."

He shook his head. "I'll be okay."

Part of me wanted to grab him and make him come home with me. But the other part knew that things had changed between us. I just didn't understand why.

"Suit yourself," I said.

He walked off.

I peered through my blue taw one more time before dropping it into my pouch. I skipped all the way home.

When I got there, Mama was setting the table. The air in the kitchen smelled like baked apples. Higgie was in the bathtub. I could hear him singing one of his nonsense songs.

"It's almost five. Where have you been?" she said.

"I had to stay after school."

Mama started in, but I held up my hand. "It wasn't only me! The whole class had to stay and work on vocabulary."

She narrowed her eyes at me. "Did Mrs. Thompson send a note home?"

I stared at the floor. "No, Mama."

"It smells good in here," I added.

"I made applesauce for dessert. Get washed up for supper. Daddy should be home any minute."

I closed the door of my room and hid the marble pouch under my bed, near the wall, promising myself I'd put the marbles back in Mama's drawer as soon as possible.

Except for the blue taw.

Chapter Fifteen
A Spooky Night

OCTOBER 31, 1959

I've almost forgiven Daddy for the night he wrecked the car. Now we share a secret. When Mama was bathing, he caught me with my hand in her dresser drawer.

He snuck up behind me. "What have you got there, Sugar Beet?"

I snatched my hand away. "I was just checking on my marbles, that's all."

He was grinning, but I felt bad. I wasn't stealing them. I was putting them back.

I'd been stealing the pouch in the afternoon and practicing my shot in the bathroom every night when I was supposed to be getting ready for bed. And every morning I'd been putting the pouch back the first chance I got.

I shuffled my feet. "Daddy, I still want to be in the

marble competition, and I've been secretly practicing."

"What if your mama catches you?" he asked.

I said, "She won't."

He ran his fingers through his hair. I could see the scar from where he'd had the stitches removed. "You know she can't be bothered with any trouble now that it's almost time for the baby."

He didn't say it, but I also knew that the entry form was in the Chevy. In the junkyard.

"Okay." My chin dipped down.

I was nearly out of the bedroom when he added, "It's as good a time as any to tell you that I'm sorry, Freedom."

I knew what he was talking about. "Thanks, Daddy."

"I'm gonna do better."

I thought about the new bottles of beer in the Frigidaire. "I know."

"Now you need to get out of here. It's almost candy time!"

Halloween night is my favorite holiday, next to Christmas. I went to my room to put on my costume. I was going to be a cat. I put on a black leotard and black tights. Mama had glued felt ears to a headband and sewn a long felt tail to the bottom half of my leotard.

I had wanted to be a lion, but she told me a lion head was too hard to make out of felt. I never said I wanted her to sew the costume. I wanted the one I'd seen hanging on the rack at Woolworth's.

I suppose it didn't matter, because I'd be wearing a coat over the whole outfit.

Everyone was in the kitchen. Mama had baked a spice cake, and it was cooling on the counter. Daddy was at the table, folding up my UNICEF box. I planned on collecting as many nickels as possible for those kids in Africa. I also hoped for lots of bubble gum in my pillowcase.

I tried not to think about how easy it'd be to get the competition fee from that UNICEF box at the end of the night. If I could even find a way to enter on my own.

"Meow!" Daddy said when he saw me.

Higgie was slapping everything in sight with his pillowcase.

"Stand still, Higgie," Mama said. She buttoned up the back of his clown outfit and helped him into his coat. I was glad to be rid of that clown costume after wearing it two years in a row. Mama had painted his nose with red lipstick like she used to do for me.

"Ready for your makeup?" Mama asked me. I stood still while she drew kitty whiskers on my face with her eyeliner pencil. I also got a black nose. It tickled as she drew it on, and I giggled.

We stood in front of the television while Mama snapped a photo. She kept calling Higgie "precious." And he kept tugging on my tail.

Precious, my eye.

You couldn't see Higgie's bright red-and-yellow costume

except for his legs, because he was bundled up so tight in his coat, scarf, hat, and gloves. His red nose was peeking out. It was already smeared.

Mama asked Higgie if he wanted to go to the bathroom one more time. She acted as if we were going on a long car ride.

"Oh, come on and let's go already," I said. "The neighbors will be out of nickels by the time we get to them."

Daddy put a nickel in my UNICEF box and shook it. "There's something to get you started."

"I'll be right here waiting," Mama said. She rubbed her belly like it was a genie's lamp.

Higgie yelled, "Let's go scare the neighbors!"

"Start with Mrs. Zierk," Mama said.

Daddy winked at Mama and pulled on his thick winter gloves. The door slammed behind us, and we were off.

The streets were covered in a light dusting of snow, and the wind was blowing. Our oak tree's branches were waving around the dark sky like skeleton fingers. A few brown leaves danced ahead of us on the sidewalk. Most of the porch lights on our neighbors' houses were glowing. Except for Mrs. Zierk's. As usual. You could see the glow coming from her old black-and-white television instead.

Higgie said, "You are walking too slow, Freedom."

Daddy chuckled as Higgie zigzagged up Mrs. Nelsen's yard and stood with a bunch of big kids waiting at the door.

Higgie yelled, "Trick or treat!" and got his candy. He

didn't even say thank you before he ran on to the next house.

I looked up at Daddy, and he said, "Go on! Get your candy!"

He waited on the sidewalk while I ran up the steps to Mrs. Nelsen's before she could shut the door. A row of jack-o'-lanterns beamed on the steps.

By the time we got to the end of Lilac Street, my pillowcase was already bulging. I had a popcorn ball, a couple of store-bought cookies wrapped in cellophane, and a rainbow lollipop along with some Smarties and Tootsie Rolls. I peered into my pillowcase. Some of it looked like old people's candy: peppermints, throat lozenges—that kind of stuff. I'd give them to Mama for her church purse. I smiled when I spied a whole pack of bubble gum near the bottom of the pillowcase. I'd have to hide it when we got home. Mama can't stand it when I blow bubbles.

I got a Tootsie Roll from Mrs. Coyle. She patted me on the head and told me to have fun and stay warm. Maybe she still likes me, after all.

We went to the last house on our street. Mr. Swanson put a quarter in my UNICEF box, but he said it was only because he wasn't giving out candy this year.

I begged Daddy for one more house, and he agreed. But we shouldn't have bothered. Most of the porch lights were already off, and a little gray-haired lady that I didn't know gave Higgie and me an apple each but no nickels for UNICEF. I had walked all that way for an apple when Mama had a bowlful at home. The icy wind was biting my cheeks. My fingers were going numb. But I wanted to collect two dollars for UNICEF, and I had only about a dollar fifty, if I'd counted right. I couldn't wait to dump out my pillowcase on the living-room floor and divvy up the loot. I planned on swapping anything I could with Higgie for his pack of bubble gum.

The wind picked up. The clouds cast a spooky haze over the neighborhood. Somewhere, a branch scraped at the side of a house. If I wasn't with my daddy, I'd have been a bit scared.

Higgie started whining.

Daddy said, "Let's go home and see what Mama has in store for us."

We always have a pot of hot cocoa on Halloween night. I also thought about that freshly baked spice cake, served with two dollops of whipped cream. Daddy would tell us a ghost story or two, and we'd get to eat some of our candy before bed.

When we rounded the corner by our house, there weren't many trick-or-treaters left. We walked by Mrs. Zierk's. I sucked in my breath when I saw her silver mailbox in pieces on the street. Someone was up to Halloween pranks.

We stopped. Sure enough, we heard giggling and rustling in the bushes around us. Daddy peered into the dark. "Who's there?" His voice was gruff.

An egg went *splat* on Mrs. Zierk's front door! I saw a shadow move in her bushes. I stared at the egg as it slid down, leaving a shiny trail of egg snot.

Another egg sailed through the air and hit the house. Daddy whirled around, yelling, "Stop that!"

Higgie grabbed for my hand. It was all I could do not to run.

Mrs. Zierk's porch light turned on, cutting a line in the darkness. Another egg went sailing over my head. It landed on her doormat.

Suddenly Mrs. Zierk was at the screen door, shouting, "Get off my property!" She shook her broom. If I didn't know better, I'd have thought she was a witch. Her hair was falling out of its bun, and her eyes were wild.

Daddy stepped into the light. "Good evening, Henrietta."

"Who's that sneaking around in my bushes? Are you throwing eggs at my house? You'd better get out of here, you hooligans! Do you hear me?"

Daddy held up his hand. "Now, Henrietta, it's probably just a couple of kids playing around."

Mrs. Zierk stood on her porch in a faded housecoat and slippers. She was sputtering and shaking.

A roll of toilet paper went sailing by and got stuck in the branches over our heads. Another landed with a *plop* on the roof, then unrolled into the gutter, leaving a trail of TP waving in the air like a flag. It would be a terrible mess to clean up.

Mrs. Zierk clutched at her shoulder and gasped. Daddy just about caught her before she fell.

Just about.

Mrs. Zierk collapsed in a heap on the steps, wheezing like an old vacuum cleaner. Her eyes were closed, and there was spittle on her lips.

Daddy put his coat around her. "Run home, Freedom! Tell your mama to call for the doctor."

I dropped my pillowcase and ran for home as fast as my nearly frozen legs could carry me.

As I burst through the door, Mama stood up from the kitchen table. "Slow down, Freedom Jane!"

"Daddy needs you at Mrs. Zierk's house!" I yelled.

Mama grabbed her coat from the hook. "Is it Higgie?"

"No, Mama. It's Mrs. Zierk. She fell down, and Daddy is trying to wake her up."

Mama knew what to do even though I was too out of breath to tell her. While she called the doctor, I waited by the stove. The oven door was ajar, so I held my hands out to warm them. My toes felt itchy and tingly in my socks. I wiggled them and looked around the kitchen. The spice cake sat uncovered. I stuck a finger in the icing and licked it, but I was so nervous, I couldn't taste it.

Poor Mrs. Zierk.

Mama hung up the phone. "Grab the blanket from the sofa, and let's go!"

Mama was off, the blanket flapping around her like bat wings. She moved quickly despite her size.

When Mama and I got next door, Mrs. Zierk was sitting up on the steps. The color was back in her face. She still had Daddy's coat around her shoulders. He must've been freezing to death without it.

Higgie started crying when he saw Mama. He was holding onto Daddy's pant leg.

I spotted Jacob and Esau Mooney sitting on the porch swing. They both had their heads down and their hands in their laps. I'd never seem them so quiet in all my life.

Higgie whispered, "Those boys got yelled at while you were gone."

I grabbed his hand. "Shush!"

Mama put the blanket around Mrs. Zierk. "Henrietta? Are you all right?"

Mrs. Zierk sighed. "Been better." Her voice was shaky.

Mama began yelling at the boys. "You are going to scrub every speck of this mess off her house, or I'll get Chief Wilson on the telephone!"

Daddy said, "Now, Willie."

"Why are you throwing eggs at her house anyhow? That's a waste of food. Are you trying to kill her?"

"No, sir. I mean, ma'am," Esau said.

Jacob said, "We're just having some fun."

"Fun? You are sure going to have fun cleaning this up."

"Yes, ma'am," said Esau.

Daddy said, "You boys better get home. Come into the house, Henrietta."

Higgie and I sat on Mrs. Zierk's sofa. Higgie kept wiggling, but I sat absolutely still. At least it was warm inside. Daddy was pacing, running his hands through his hair.

Higgie leaned up against my arm. "I want to go home," he said.

I was too worried to think. There was a knock at the front door. Daddy let in Doc Brooks. The doc took off his hat. "What happened?"

"She says it's probably her heart," Daddy explained.

"Is she going to be okay?" I asked. I realized how much I'd miss Mrs. Zierk if she didn't live next door.

"The doctor here will fix her right up," Daddy said.

I peeked through the bedroom doorway at Mrs. Zierk, who was lying down with Mama at her side. She looked so small in her big wrought iron bed. Mama had piled four blankets on top of her.

"Let's go home," Daddy said. "Mama is going to stay the night. She'll call if there's any news."

Higgie jumped into Daddy's arms. I wasn't sure I wanted to leave, but I was awful tired.

As we trudged home, I asked, "How come Mama always says bad things about Mrs. Zierk but helped her tonight?"

Daddy said, "Good neighbors help each other in times of trouble, no matter what."

"Yes, but Mama hates Mrs. Zierk. Doesn't she?"

Daddy stared down at me. "Freedom, your mama has a heart of gold, even though she can't show it all the time. Her parents were real tough on her. She's doing the best she can." He stopped and put his hand on the top of my head. "That's all any of us can do."

I thought for a moment. Mrs. Zierk needed Mama tonight. And maybe Mama needed Mrs. Zierk. "So, Mama's got a hard shell on the outside, but she's really soft in the middle? Like M&M's?"

He squeezed my hand. "That's right, Sugar Beet. Mama is like an M&M. And sometimes she can be so sweet. Can't she?"

I thought about hot cocoa and spice cake and my cat costume—and how Mama had looked while she was tending to Mrs. Zierk in the bedroom—and for once I didn't argue. "Yep."

Chapter Sixteen
A Meeting of Minds

NOVEMBER 8, 1959

This morning Mama wasn't feeling well. She'd mixed up a coffee cake at 6:00 but had gone back to bed while it was baking. She was hot when the rest of us were cold, and her nose wouldn't stop running. Her ankles were swollen. She'd tossed and turned all night with a wet washcloth over her face. She said she was sick of being pregnant.

"Your mama is simply worn out," Daddy told me.

It turned out that Mrs. Zierk had herself a mild heart attack on Halloween. That night Mama practically adopted our neighbor, and we've been feeding her and waiting on her hand and foot ever since. Seems like Mama is always sending me over there with something: cookies, tea bags, soup, carrot cake, newspapers, and more.

Mrs. Zierk has to be feeling better by now. I know she's awful strong—and clever. If you ask me, she's acting frail to get free help for as long as she can.

The Meanie brothers have been raking leaves, shoveling snow, cleaning out gutters, and helping her with anything and everything else she needs done. Daddy says that Mama has them "in her back pocket" as long as she doesn't call Chief Wilson about what they did that night.

Yesterday Daddy built a new mailbox for Mrs. Zierk. He also sweeps off her steps every evening. It must have something to do with Mrs. Zierk being "alone in the world." I heard Mama telling Aunt Janie that.

Funny how it never bothered her before. But then, she never really got to know Mrs. Zierk.

I got ready for church all by myself today. Well, Daddy zipped me up, but that's it. I even did my own hair. I parted it on the side and clipped it with a tiny barrette. My hair looked real shiny because I'd brushed it until all the poodle curls calmed down. I was wearing a pale pink dress with my polished-up saddle shoes.

The whole kitchen smelled like burnt coffee grounds since Daddy ruined the coffee this morning. I wrinkled my nose while I ate my Sugar Crisps. Higgie threw his bowl of oatmeal on the floor.

Daddy told Higgie he was done with breakfast. "But don't you move from that seat!"

Higgie whined, "Why can't I get down?" His hair was

sticking up in the back, and pieces of oatmeal were stuck all over his neck. I tried smoothing down his hair, but he pushed my hands away.

"Because I have to get this cleaned up before you track it all over the house." Daddy wiped oatmeal from the floor with one of Mama's fancy dish towels while Higgie pouted.

When Mama waddled into the kitchen, I waited for the yelling. It's a good thing she was too distracted to see what Daddy was doing with the fancy dish towel. She put on her oven mitts and took the coffee cake out of the stove, setting it on the counter to cool. Daddy tossed the towel toward the sink, then settled in at the kitchen table with his own bowl of Sugar Crisps and the newspaper.

Mama came over and touched my head. "Your hair sure looks nice, Freedom."

I blushed. "I did it myself."

She went to the drawer by the phone and handed me a package.

Higgie tugged on Mama's housecoat. "Where's my present?"

Mama bent slowly and kissed him. "Go find your Bible, Higgie." He scampered from the room.

Inside the package, I found a new pair of white gloves.

I smiled. "Thank you, Mama."

I knew better than to try them on while I was eating. I drank the milk from my cereal bowl and went to rinse it out. Mama leaned into the counter and rubbed at her lower back. She sighed.

"Are you all right, Mama?" I asked.

"I'm fine. I'm probably too big to fit in my church dress, that's all." She wrapped a piece of coffee cake in a clean dish towel and told me to take it over to Mrs. Zierk. "Don't diddle dawdle. Just take it over and come back so we can get to the service on time for once. And don't you dare get dirty."

Mama poured herself a glass of milk and went to her room to dress. My smile disappeared. I had planned on being ladylike all day long. She never trusts me. I sneaked a look at Daddy. He winked at me over the sports page. He looked so handsome in his blue suit. His eyes were clear and bright.

He hasn't been drinking at all since Halloween night.

I kissed Daddy on the cheek. His aftershave was musky under my lips. I put my arms around his neck and whispered, "Can I sit by you in church today?"

"Does that mean you've truly forgiven me?" he asked.

"Yes, Daddy, I have."

"I'm trying real hard, Freedom."

"I know."

"I've gone to three meetings this week."

"I'm glad." I didn't know what else to say.

He rubbed his chin. "Well, you'd better get over there with that coffee cake before she has to tell you again."

I put on my coat over my church outfit. The sleeves were getting too short.

He winked again as I shut the back door. I avoided the

muddy parts of the yard all the way over to Mrs. Zierk's house. I knocked on her door and waited. She didn't come right away, so I peeked in the window.

Mrs. Zierk was standing in the living room in front of the mirror. She looked dressed up, and she was pinning a hat to her hair.

I knocked again.

This time she answered. "Good morning, Freedom."

"Where are you going?" I asked.

"I was thinking I might go to church with your family this morning. To say thank you to the good Lord for giving me a few more days on this wretched Earth."

She put the coffee cake in the bread box. My mouth hung open while she pulled on her gloves. Mrs. Zierk never goes to church. And I mean *never*.

She slipped into some sturdy black shoes. "Close your mouth, Freedom. Now, where's my purse?"

I pointed to the big black pocketbook on her kitchen counter.

"Aha!" She looped the straps around her wrist. "Do you think your parents would mind if I rode in your car?"

"I guess not."

We walked back to my house in silence. I hid a smile behind my hand. If I planned it right, there'd be at least two whole people sitting between Higgie and me at church. Then I wouldn't have any trouble during the service.

Mama was standing on the porch. I could tell she wanted to start in on me for dawdling. But instead she smiled at

Mrs. Zierk. "Henrietta, don't you look lovely this morning. Where are you off to?"

When Mrs. Zierk asked if she could come to church with us, Mama's chest puffed out with pride, like God was going to save us a spot in heaven just because Mrs. Zierk asked to ride in our new old car.

"Why, of course we have room for you."

Higgie came bouncing out of the house and nearly knocked us over. Mama put out her hands to hold him back. She yelled over her shoulder, "Homer, get in the car!" Mama licked her fingers and smoothed down Higgie's cowlick. "Come on, Freedom. You, too."

There was a scraping sound when Mrs. Zierk climbed into the backseat. I wondered if the new old car could hold all of us. I hopped in next to her and pulled the door shut.

The DeSoto still smelled, but Mrs. Zierk didn't seem to mind. "What's your pastor's name again?" she asked.

Mama got settled in the front and said, "Pastor Davis." Her belly almost touched the glove box. Higgie was squished in the middle of the front seat. He fiddled with the radio until Mama stopped him.

Mrs. Zierk said, "Didn't his wife run off last year?"

That's all it took for Mama to start gossiping. "Why, yes, she did. . . ."

The engine roared. I waited for Daddy to say "We're off like a turd of hurdles," but he couldn't get a word in edgewise. He had the biggest grin on his face while he pulled out of the driveway.

We were too late for Bible school, but I got to sit between Daddy and Mrs. Zierk during the service. Mama sat next to Mrs. Zierk. Higgie was all the way on the other side of Mama. Mrs. Zierk mumbled along with the singing portion and put a whopping five dollars in the collection plate. I got to put in a nickel. I didn't get into trouble once, but Higgie got tapped twice by the thimble.

After church Mrs. Zierk said hello to everyone she knew while we waited by the car.

Daddy was hungry, and Mama was getting a headache.

"Where is that woman?" Daddy asked.

I saw Mrs. Zierk making her way through a group of people. "Here she comes."

"Don't point, Freedom Jane," Mama said.

The car doors squeaked open, and we all got in. "Well, do you have plans for lunch?" Mrs. Zierk asked.

"I've got two pounds of ground beef thawing in the sink," Mama said. "At sixty-one cents a pound, there's no need to waste it."

"I thought it would be nice to go out for lunch," Mrs. Zierk said. I saw Mama holding her breath until Mrs. Zierk added, "My treat."

"That would be real nice," Daddy replied before Mama could say no.

I'd never been to a restaurant in my whole life! I mean, I've had a grilled cheese or a chocolate malted at the counter at Woolworth's, but Mama and Daddy never take us out.

The grown-ups decided on the diner on Third Street.

As soon as we sat down in the red Naugahyde booth, Higgie announced, "My mama's got a baby in that big, fat belly!"

I snickered behind my glossy menu.

Mama shushed him, and Mrs. Zierk said, "It's not nice to discuss that in mixed company, Higginbotham."

The waitress put a glass of water and some silverware in front of each of us.

Higgie said, "I have to go potty."

Daddy took him by the hand and led him away.

Mrs. Zierk turned to me. "You must be getting excited about the marble-shooting thingamajig next weekend." She leaned in close. "Shooting marbles with a pack of boys seems like a fun challenge for a girl your age. I just know you'll win the grand prize. Isn't it a hundred dollars?" Her eyes sparkled. She knew darn well about my struggles with Mama over marbles.

I realized what she was doing. I took a deep breath and played along. "Mama hasn't actually decided if I'm allowed to enter."

Mama looked up from her menu. "I told you, Freedom. I don't think it's a good idea."

Mrs. Zierk turned to Mama. "Why not?"

She had Mama in the hot seat.

"It's just that . . ." Mama paused. "Well, honestly, Henrietta, it's not right to encourage competition between girls and boys."

"Pish posh!" Mrs. Zierk said. "That's the silliest thing

I've ever heard. You should let her enter, Wilhelmina. It will be good for her."

I burst out, "Girls can do anything boys can do!"

Mrs. Zierk sat back and smiled. "It's settled. Freedom will be in the competition!"

I waited for Mama to argue.

"I'm always proud of you, Freedom." Mama sighed. "I suppose you could enter. Just this once."

I squealed and hugged my mother with all my might. "Oh, Mama, I'll make you even prouder. I promise."

"Don't go spilling your water, Freedom Jane!" I let go of her, and she reached for my wobbly glass.

Daddy came back with Higgie. "What are you ladies talking about?"

"Oh, nothing," Mama said.

Higgie and I shared a plate of spaghetti. I ate two pieces of garlic toast and a salad with Italian dressing. Everyone had a chocolate sundae with a cherry on top for dessert—even Mama. The whole time, I marveled at how sneaky Mrs. Zierk got Mama to change her mind.

Right before bed, Mama gave me back my marble pouch. I took the pouch from her and stuffed it under my pillow. "How come you're letting me enter?"

She smoothed my curls. "Seems it's not up to me to stop you. You won't give up until you try."

I fell asleep with a smile on my face.

Chapter Seventeen
How You Play the Game

NOVEMBER 14, 1959

It was the most wonderful day for an Autumn Jubilee! An overnight snow had melted, and the golden sun peeked through the billowy clouds. We were standing on Capital Avenue, watching the Jubilee festivities. Higgie was up on Daddy's shoulders while I held Daddy's warm hand. Mama sat in a lawn chair in between Uncle Mort and Aunt Janie. Aunt Janie looked glamorous in a fur coat and dark sunglasses.

The air smelled of fresh popcorn and apple cider.

Uncle Mort was drinking something from a bottle wrapped in a brown paper bag. He took a big swig.

I held my breath when he offered a sip to Daddy. Mama frowned.

"Naw, I'm saving myself for a root beer," Daddy said.

Mama smiled. I let out my breath.

She'd allowed me to wear my jeans, and I had rolled each leg up to my ankle. "Just for the competition," Mama said. I had my marble pouch in my coat pocket and could barely wait until noon.

The Jubilee always opens with a parade, and it started right on time.

The Jubilee Princess led the way in a pink-and-white Skyliner convertible. Her two ladies-in-waiting wore matching pink chiffon dresses, and they all waved from their pink tissue-flowered chariot. I coveted one of those dresses. I couldn't help it.

Higgie was wearing his cowboy hat and spurs. He made shooting noises and pointed at people with his finger. Daddy had bought him a rubber band gun from a street vendor, but Higgie ran out of rubber bands in about five minutes.

"Need more," he whined. But Mama said no. Then she put the gun in her purse.

Mrs. Zierk walked by. She was wearing a fancy velvet hat and her Sunday best. When she saw our family, she stopped to say hello.

"It's nice to see you out and about," said Mama. "Why don't you join us here on the curb?"

Mrs. Zierk said, "If I sit down, I might not be able to get up again." She tipped her hat. "See you over at the park, Freedom." She looked hard at Higgie. "Higginbotham."

Mrs. Zierk walked away, nodding at people as she went,

including my teacher. Mrs. Thompson was holding a man's hand. I didn't even know she had three little girls, but there was her family, perched on the sidelines like us.

The war veterans marched by, and Higgie cheered like crazy. Horses pranced with their long manes and swishy tails. I wished I could ride one of them sidesaddle like Dale Evans on TV. But I have to say, the horses were a bit smelly, and I was glad when they passed. Colorful clowns strolled by. And a juggler. Some dogs were dressed like clowns, too.

Mama said, "Aren't they precious?"

Nancy waved at me from across the street. She was with her mama, who was looking well. I was glad to see that Mrs. Brown was feeling better, but I couldn't go over to say hi. Mama was too scared I'd get lost in the crowd. Besides, the first of the floats was already in sight.

Daddy put Higgie down. "You're getting heavy, son. Now, hold your sister's hand and don't run off."

My brother's hand was sticky, so I dropped it the minute Daddy looked away. "Here they come, Higgie!" I pointed down the street.

Each parade float was more elaborate than the last. Teenagers on top threw candy, and all the kids went scrambling for it. I sprinted to the middle of the street and scooped some up.

Mama yelled, "Don't get run over!"

I came back to the curb with two rolls of Smarties and a grape lollipop. I gave Higgie the lollipop and tucked the Smarties in my pocket for later.

The high school band stopped and marched in place while they played "My Country 'Tis of Thee." I felt so proud. When they got to the part about me, I belted out the words: "Let *freedom* ring!"

The band marched on, and I waved as the last of the parade went by.

I should have known the day was too good to be true.

Mama peered down at me and asked, "Where's Higgie? You were supposed to be watching him."

Daddy said, "That rascal must have run off."

Mama gasped.

Aunt Janie patted her arm. "Oh, I'm sure he's close by."

But I knew better. I've seen how much trouble Higgie can get into in five minutes.

The street was emptying out. All of the other families were headed over to the park with their picnic baskets.

Mama cried, "I hope he isn't playing near the falls like last time!"

I shuddered. The "terrible incident."

We'd gone to Tautphaus Park last Fourth of July for a family picnic. Daddy had made boats out of newspaper for us to float down Snake River and over the falls. Higgie had wanted to keep his boat, but I'd launched it anyway. And when he reached for the boat, he fell in.

Headfirst.

Daddy snatched him up right away, but it scared Mama silly. I couldn't believe the size of the crowd that gathered that day. We were practically famous. Nothing that exciting ever happens in Idaho Falls.

And that is why we can't ever go near Snake River by ourselves.

Higgie wouldn't dare go near the falls again. Would he? Suddenly, I had an idea. "I'll bet he's at the duck pond!"

Higgie loves the duck pond. Daddy takes us there to feed the ducks and geese from a loaf of day-old bread.

Mama wrung her hands. Daddy said, "Maybe you're right, Freedom. Let's go have a look-see."

Aunt Janie said, "Shouldn't we call someone?"

"We'll find him," Uncle Mort replied.

Mama was pale. I knew she was worried out of her mind. Why did I let go of his hand?

Daddy took Mama's arm. "It's going to be all right, Willie."

We all walked over together. My eyes scanned the pond. I saw a family sitting on a blanket. There was a couple walking hand in hand. Two geese waddled by.

Mama had to sit down because she felt faint.

And there Higgie was—fast asleep on a bench!

"Good thinking, Freedom," Uncle Mort said. He took off his hat and wiped his forehead with his hankie. I patted his arm, even though he smelled like beer.

Higgie looked like a dirty angel, all curled up in a ball, with his thumb hanging out of his mouth. I almost wanted to hug him. Mama grabbed him so hard, she could have crushed him. She didn't seem to care that his pants were wet and his feet were muddy.

He rubbed his eyes. "I fell asleep."

"Shush now." She cuddled him the best she could around her baby belly.

"Freedom?" she shouted.

I jumped.

Mama looked at her watch and stood up quickly. "We've got to get over to the marble competition!"

The competition area was all the way over by the playground. I could see people gathering at the judges' table. We'd almost missed it!

Aunt Janie took Higgie from Mama. "I'll take Higgin-botham home."

Mama told him to be good. Then she nodded at me. "Let's go."

Daddy asked me, "Are you ready to become the Marble Queen?"

I patted the coat pocket that held my marble pouch. "I'm ready!"

We hurried over to the judges' table, where I filled out a late entry form. Daddy paid the fee with two wrinkled dollar bills from his wallet. "I've been saving up. You can pay me back when you win this thing, Freedom."

Of course, I was the only girl in line. I saw the Meanie brothers and Anthony, but there was no sign of Daniel. I was disappointed for some reason.

Mama leaned over and whispered, "Are you sure you

want to do this, Freedom?"

I met her eyes and bobbed my head. "More than anything."

She smiled a mysterious smile. "All righty then. Go show the boys in this town a thing or two about marble shooting."

There were two official rings, and only sixteen of us had shown up to play. I guess marble shooting isn't as popular as it used to be.

I stood in the lag line next to Wally Biscotti.

"Aw, nuts. They're really letting *you* play?" he said.

I elbowed him in the side. "You bet."

When Esau walked over and said "Good luck, Freedom," I felt his gaze all the way to my toes.

I took out my blue taw and warmed it up on my leg. As the judges rattled off the rules, my mouth went dry. We were playing Sudden Death. One loss and I'd be out of the competition. Each player would be listed on a tournament bracket according to lag throw.

I was so nervous I thought I might be sick. I sneaked a look at my family. Uncle Mort was grinning. Daddy was, too.

Finally it was time to throw lag. Esau threw the farthest. I bungled mine and came in ninth. The judges wrote our names on the official brackets. I couldn't stop fidgeting. They taped the brackets to the judges' table, and I found my name. I was signed up to play in Ring Two. I'd be competing in the first game against a kid I didn't know.

The two of us threw a quick lag, and I was first. The referee set up the cross in the middle of the ring, and I bent down to shoot. The people around us crowded in too close. The referee shouted, "Give these mibsters some room!"

There wasn't even time to pray. I blew on my taw and flipped it into the ring.

I got seven marbles in two shots. We weren't playing for keepsies, but that kid had tears in his eyes when I beat him.

We shook hands. "Good match," I told him.

Esau had won his first game in Ring One. I'm sure he beat the kid easy.

I sat out for games two, three, and four, just watching the other matches. Wally Biscotti lost right away. His daddy grabbed him by the ear after his game. They didn't even stick around to watch the rest.

Anthony won his first game but lost his next one.

Mama made me eat a sandwich from the picnic basket. I drank some root beer and paced around on the grass.

In my second game I was paired up with a kid from school. I won by two marbles. Then I sat out again. My feet were getting cold, and I had to go to the bathroom.

Jacob won his first match. But he lost his next game to a kid who looked even tougher than he did. He pouted and stormed off.

I was set to play that tough kid in my third game. If I were playing him in the school yard, I would have been afraid. He was at least fifteen.

It had started to drizzle. We threw lag, and the tough kid won. I put my hands in my pockets to warm up my fingers.

The kid cracked his knuckles and sneered at me. "I'm gonna clean up this ring, girl." His black hair was greasy, and his breath stank.

My heart beat in my ears.

When he knuckled down in the cold mud, he flinched, and his taw bounced out without hitting a thing. It was my turn.

I looked over at my family. Mama had been pacing around all afternoon without resting much in the lawn chair that Daddy had set up for her. Nancy and her mama and Mrs. Zierk had joined them. Uncle Mort had given Mrs. Zierk his lawn chair. I stared at Daddy.

"Focus," Daddy mouthed.

So I did.

And I was the one who cleaned up the ring. My family clapped and cheered. I kind of wished Higgie were there.

I didn't want to shake hands with that greasy-haired kid, but I did it anyway.

By 4:00 there were only three of us left.

The air had grown colder, and the crowd had thinned.

Over in the other ring I watched while Esau played against another kid I didn't know. I chewed my thumbnail clear to the skin as I watched them battle it out.

Esau won by two marbles.

I would be playing Esau Mooney for the championship!

The refs rushed us along because of the weather. I didn't

even have time to get a drink or go to the bathroom before the final game.

Esau winked at me as we gathered at the ring. We threw lag. Esau threw farther and got to shoot first. He knocked out two marbles and missed on the next shot.

I closed my eyes and cradled my blue taw for a moment before I took my turn. The wind had picked up. And the rain, too. Truth be told, playing marbles in the rain wasn't much fun. My eyelashes were nearly frozen to my face.

Mama looked like she was holding her breath—along with her belly. I knew she needed to get home.

I ignored the rain and the mud and everything else and knuckled down. I knocked out three marbles. And missed my next shot. It was Esau's turn again.

He knuckled down and put a fancy spin on his shot. I closed my eyes. The crowd started cheering.

When I opened my eyes again, I saw my fate: He'd won the championship.

There was clapping and shouting and whistling. In the middle of it all, I reached for Esau's hand. "Good game."

He shrugged and bent his head close to mine. "You sure are a good mibster, Freedom. It could've been either of us."

We waited for the referee and the judges to make the announcement. I couldn't look at my family now. They had to be disappointed in me. The grand prize would have helped Mama to buy some things for the baby and who knows what else.

And I wasn't the Marble Queen.

A judge went to the microphone stand. "Folks! Folks!" He waved for everyone to be quiet. "Mr. William Shaw, publisher of the *Post Register*, will be announcing the winner of the 1959 Autumn Jubilee Marble-Shooting Competition."

He picked up a bronze trophy of a boy marble player from the judges' table and handed it to a man wearing a thick black coat and a tall hat.

Mr. William Shaw shouted into the microphone, "Let the record show: Freedom Jane McKenzie is the runner-up. And Esau Mooney is the 1959 Marble King of Idaho Falls! Come up and get your prizes, kids. Courtesy of the *Post Register*, your local newspaper."

I didn't know there was going to be a prize for runner-up.

Esau clutched a crisp hundred-dollar bill in one hand and the trophy in the other while he posed for pictures.

I collected twenty-five dollars from a judge and watched while Esau was congratulated by Mr. William Shaw and the judges and referee.

"Let's get an official photograph for the front page," a man with a camera said. "Shake hands, mibsters."

Esau put his money in his pocket. He held out his hand, and I squeezed it. We turned to look at the photographer. A flashbulb popped. And I saw stars.

Daddy picked me up and spun me around. "Whoo-hoo!" he yelled.

Uncle Mort said, "You played good."

Nancy said, "That sure was exciting!"

Mrs. Zierk patted my shoulder. "Nice job, Freedom!"

Mama just beamed.

"But I didn't win," I told them.

"It's not about winning. It's how you play the game!" Mrs. Zierk declared.

I could tell Mama was tired, but she said, "Shall we go for ice cream to celebrate?"

"Naw, let's go home and tell Higgie all about it," I said.

While we walked to the car, Mama announced "That's my girl!" to everyone we passed.

The rain turned to fat snowflakes just as Daddy started up the new old car.

Chapter Eighteen
Oh, Baby!

NOVEMBER 23, 1959

Mama let me keep ten dollars from my marble winnings. She put the rest in the bank.

"For your future education," she told me.

My picture was in the paper. Underneath, it said: Esau Mooney, Marble King, and Freedom McKenzie, Runner-up. It looks like we're holding hands instead of shaking. I'm blushing. You can tell, even though the photograph is black-and-white. Daddy must've bought up twenty papers.

I bought new roller skates and some wax lips for Higgie. On the Sunday after the competition, I put a whole dollar in the collection plate.

Daniel's mother called from work and asked if he could eat with us tonight. Mama said yes, but she was grumbling about an extra mouth to feed as soon as she got off the phone. She asked me to call Daniel.

I was reading in the living room. "Can't you call him?"

Mama had her cookbook out on the table. She was making a grocery list for our Thanksgiving feast in two days. She had told me that I could bake the pumpkin pie by myself.

"Freedom! He's your friend," Mama said, rubbing her belly. It looked as if it were going to pop at any second. The baby was late.

"Used-to-be friend, Mama."

"Call him," she said, and hurried into the bathroom.

I stood in the kitchen staring at my fingernails while I waited for the operator to put the call through.

He finally answered on the fourth ring. "Hello?"

"Hi, Daniel. It's me, Freedom."

"What do you want?"

"You have to come over for supper. Your mother is working late tonight, doing inventory."

"I'm fine right here."

I stomped my foot. "Daniel, don't you dare get me into trouble. My mama says to come over."

There was only silence on the other end of the line.

"Daniel?"

"What?"

"You can bring your marbles, and we can shoot on the rug like old times."

He hung up on me!

When I got back to the living room, Higgie was sitting in the fuzzy green rocker. I pulled on his arm. "I was sitting there!"

Higgie swatted me away. "Not anymore!"

I almost flicked him on the head, but then I remembered. Christmas was only weeks away. I didn't need to get on Santa's naughty list.

I settled for the floor in front of the television. I stared at the clock. It was almost five. Mama would be putting supper on the table soon.

I waited and waited. There was a soft knock at the front door. When I opened it, I saw Daniel. He had snow in his hair and a scowl on his face.

Mama put on a big smile and handed him a towel. He took off his coat. "Wipe your feet, please," she cooed. "Supper's almost done."

I narrowed my eyes at her back while she waddled into the kitchen. I didn't smell any food cooking in there. The table wasn't even set yet. What were we going to eat? And where?

Daniel and I sat side by side on the sofa, but he acted like I wasn't even in the room. I said, "Didn't you bring your marbles?"

"Nope, I traded them for two *Archie* comic books."

"All of them?"

"Yep."

I couldn't believe it. He worked on some arithmetic homework with one eye on the television. I couldn't stop wiggling my feet.

Higgie got up and bounced against Daniel's arm. I sneaked over to the rocker and sat down.

Daniel told Higgie, "Stop that."

Higgie said, "Make me." He danced around the living room with his blanket over his head.

Daniel looked at me. "I'm sure glad I'm an only child."

Mama came out of the kitchen. "I've got a surprise. Daddy's over at the high school, helping to fix the boiler. You kids are going to have Swanson dinners in front of the TV. My back hurts. I'm going to take a hot bath."

I was amazed. We never get to eat frozen dinners.

"Daniel, would you set up the TV trays? They're in the hall closet."

"Yes, ma'am," he said.

Oh sure, he had plenty of smiles for my mama.

I didn't move from the rocker to help him. I just watched as Daniel set up the trays. "You're in the way," I said. "Show's starting."

Higgie was lying under his blanket on the floor. Mama brought out a stack of aluminum-covered trays. Higgie and I were having turkey and mashed potatoes. Daniel was going to have Mama's TV dinner, which was meat loaf.

He smiled at Mama again. "I love meat loaf, Mrs. McKenzie."

She patted him on the head. "I thought you might. I've got Twinkies for dessert."

I gave her the eye. "Twinkies? When do we ever have Twinkies?" I said. "You have all this stuff hidden in the kitchen, but we never get to have it?"

"Hush, Freedom," Mama said. "I always put Twinkies in your daddy's lunch. You know about his sweet tooth."

When she brought out our glasses of milk, she nudged Higgie on the floor. "Higgie, you asleep already?"

He sat up and yawned. He can be such a phony.

Mama helped him up. "Sit here and eat your turkey. Then you can go to bed."

"I don't want to go to bed!" Higgie cried.

I had to cut up Higgie's turkey for him. I sat back down to eat mine, but my glass tipped over and drowned my TV dinner. I would've eaten it to avoid trouble with Mama, but she came out with the Twinkies and saw the mess.

Mama frowned. "I guess you'll have a ham sandwich."

Daniel had gobbled up his meal before I even got my sandwich.

She brought it out to me and said, "I'll be in the bathroom."

Daniel licked the cream from the middle of his Twinkie. "I saw your picture in the paper," he mumbled.

"Yep." I looked at him. "I missed seeing you at the competition."

"Well, I meant what I said about being done with

marbles. I'm going to play football. Maybe get a scholarship and go to college."

"So?"

He chewed on the inside of his lip. "So, I guess I'm sorry."

"For what?"

"I wasn't nice to you all the time we were friends."

I nodded.

"You're pretty good at marbles, for a girl. The Mooney brothers said so when you weren't around. I think Esau is sweet on you."

I grinned. "I know."

Daniel dug around in his pocket and put something on the edge of my TV tray. It was his shooter.

"What's that for?"

"I thought you might want it," he said.

I put the orange-and-white striped taw up to my eye, but I couldn't see through it. The middle was murky. It had a tiny chip, probably from Bombsies. It was a gift, though. And Mama's rule is, always say thank you for a present.

"Playing marbles won't be as much fun without you. But thanks."

We watched the rest of *Bonanza*. Higgie fell asleep for real.

When the show ended, Daniel whispered, "I'd still like to be friends, if you want."

"Sure," I said. "But Nancy is my friend, too."

"I know." Daniel opened his arithmetic book. "It's okay

to have more than one friend. We'll always be friends. And neighbors."

"Yep." I stared at him. His face looked a little red. He might've been embarrassed, or maybe it was only the glow from the television.

Mama was still in the bath, so I cleared away the tinfoil plates while Daniel put away the TV trays. We didn't talk much after that.

When Daniel's mama came to pick him up, I said to him, "See you at school tomorrow."

He put on his coat. "Tell your mama thank you for dinner."

After they left I sat in the chair by the window and peeked between the curtains. A light snow was falling. I watched as Daniel offered his mama his arm as they walked across the street. At least they had each other. But I'd be lonely without my daddy. Maybe even having a mean daddy like Nancy's is better than no daddy. I can't imagine life without Higgie, either.

Daniel helped his mama up the icy stairs to their front porch. He unlocked the door with the key he keeps on a string around his neck and held it open for her. She kissed the top of his head and pointed at the steps.

She went in. A light turned on inside their house. The yellow beam spread out into the yard. Daniel tipped his face up at the sky for a moment. He caught a snowflake on his tongue. Then he reached for the shovel and started clearing the snow off the steps, just like Daddy does. He shivered but kept going.

When he was finished, he leaned the shovel up against the house and went inside to join his mother. I let the curtains fall back into place.

I knocked on the bathroom door. "Higgie's asleep in front of the TV. Mama? Are you okay?"

A shaky voice came from inside. "I'm fine, Freedom. Go on to bed."

I put myself to bed without brushing my teeth.

In the early morning hours, Daddy woke me. "Freedom, it's time for Mama to go to the hospital."

I rubbed the sleep from my eyes and started to get up, but Daddy tucked the covers around me. "There's a lot of snow out there. Stay in bed. Mrs. Zierk is on her way over to sit with you."

He went to Mama in the hallway. "It's all right, Freedom," she said. "Homer, start the car."

I heard the click of the front door. Car doors slammed, the engine rumbled, and then it was quiet. So quiet. All I could hear was my brother's slow, sleeping breaths in the bed beside mine. Daddy must have carried him in during the night.

A few minutes later Mrs. Zierk poked her head in. "I'm here," she whispered. "I'll be on the couch."

I pulled the covers up to my chin and lay there, wondering if I was getting another brother or a sister.

I decided that either one was fine by me. As long as Mama was all right.

Chapter Nineteen

Every Queen Needs a Crown

DECEMBER 25, 1959

Mama was already tired of Christmas. Strands of tinsel and bits of wrapping paper were all over the carpet. The Christmas tree's branches sagged from the weight of the colored balls and lights. We'd opened our presents bright and early.

Perry Como sang on the radio. My belly was full from our Christmas breakfast of pancakes and bacon. Daddy had the instruction manual for his new Polaroid camera in his hand, and I was sitting on the floor with my new Etch A Sketch. It didn't matter which way I turned the dials, I couldn't figure out how to draw anything on the silver screen.

Mama had taken one look at the dried-up tree this morning and said she wanted to buy a plastic tree next year. Ever since Daddy brought it home and set it in the stand, Higgie had been lying under the Christmas tree, looking up through the branches. I didn't care if our tree was half dead. It was still beautiful, and I wasn't ready for Christmas to be over yet.

Mama had put the turkey in the oven at the crack of dawn. Every single burner on the stove was going. She was boiling potatoes, sautéing onions, and letting the bread dough rise. Mrs. Zierk and Uncle Mort and Aunt Janie were coming at two for Christmas dinner. We were having two kinds of pie—my pumpkin and an apple from Mrs. Zierk—and I had helped Mama with the bread pudding.

We'd attended a special piano recital the night before at our church. Mrs. Zierk entertained a packed house with Christmas songs. Then, for the last song, she'd called Mama up to the piano! I couldn't believe my eyes when my mother walked to the front of the church.

My mama sang "Ave Maria" in front of the whole congregation. They'd been practicing without telling a single person of their plans.

The song made me cry. I can't say why exactly, but it had that effect on other people, too. Even Daddy had to wipe tears from his cheeks when Mama took her bow.

I never realized how powerful Mama's beautiful singing voice could be. I was so proud.

Mama came out of the bedroom holding my newborn sister, Barbara Jean McKenzie.

"Freedom, will you hold the baby?" she asked.

I took my sister in my arms. She was wrapped in a pink blanket and smelled like baby powder. She stared up at me with her dark blue eyes. She's cute and bald, and her toes are too long. Like mine.

Mama leaned over and kissed Daddy.

He grabbed her hand. "Can you believe we're at the end of a decade again? It'll be 1960 this time next week."

Mama sighed. "I don't want to think about that right now."

She was worn out. Little baby Barbara doesn't sleep at night. Mama is constantly warming bottles at the stove. And who knew a new baby could make so much dirty laundry? The washing machine is always running. And I am always folding undershirts and nightgowns at the kitchen table. A pail of stinky cloth diapers has taken up residence in the corner of the bathroom.

"Sit a minute with us, Willie," Daddy begged.

"Just let me get the potatoes mashed, Homer." She kissed him again.

Higgie was napping under the tree. I nudged my brother gently with my foot. "Higgie. Wake up." He was wearing new cowboy pajamas with his new cowboy boots.

"What?" He groaned.

"Get up and pick up some of the wrapping paper."

"I can't," Higgie said. "You do it."

"I'm holding Barbara," I told him.

I liked it that my new sister needed me.

"Never mind the mess," Daddy said. He was admiring a silver ball-point pen. I gave it to him and bought it with my own money, too. The striped afghan I'd made for Mama was hanging off the back of the fuzzy green rocker.

"Oh, Freedom," she'd gushed as she opened my gift. "I can't believe you made this all by yourself." Mrs. Zierk had helped me finish it off, but I knitted the whole thing. Mama doesn't seem to mind that it's a bit itchy. She covers up with it when she rocks Barbara.

My baby sister had fallen asleep in my arms. I nuzzled the top of her warm head before putting her down in the playpen. I'd known her for only a few weeks, but it felt like I'd loved her a lifetime already, even if she kept the entire house awake with her screams.

Daddy reached for me. "Come here, Sugar Beet."

I climbed up onto his lap just like I used to when I was little. He whispered, "I've got a secret something for you."

"Another present?" I exclaimed. "I got eight presents already!"

It's true. I got two records. A new pair of roller skates. A beautiful blue bicycle. A pink wool coat. A white purse to replace my black scuffed-up one. The Etch A Sketch. And a strand of seed pearls, just like the real ones Daddy had given Mama on Christmas Eve. It seems like we have more money now that Daddy doesn't drink anymore.

Daddy pointed to the tree. "You'll have to lie next to Higgie to find your present."

I scrambled over to Higgie. "Shove over."

As soon as I was on my back and looking up into the tree, I saw it. There was a silver crown nestled in the uppermost branches. I pulled the crown free, and dry needles flew everywhere.

It was a crown of marbles!

"Every queen needs a crown," Daddy said.

He'd made a crown out of a strip of sheet metal. He'd sanded it smooth and glued some of my marbles to it—like jewels.

Daddy smiled. "Try it on."

"I want one! I want a crown, too," Higgie said.

"I'll let you try it on, Higgie. After me." I put the crown on my head. It fit perfectly. "Thank you, Daddy! Thank you."

As I admired myself in the hall mirror, I thought about the competition. How important it had been for me to win, but then how it felt okay, even meant to be, when I'd lost to Esau. I hadn't felt like playing marbles all month.

You know how sometimes you need to do something—especially when people say you can't, you have to try anyway? Well, that's how I felt about marble shooting. I'd done it. And maybe it was time to try something else.

Mama came out of the kitchen and saw me wearing the crown.

"That's real nice," she said.

Daddy snapped a photo of us with his new Polaroid. When the picture came out of the opening in the front, he waved it around until the image appeared.

I stared at Mama and me. We both looked happy.

Daddy clapped his hands. "Okay, time for cleaning up."

I offered Higgie my crown. "You can wear it while we clean."

When Higgie is a little older, I'll give him the pouch with the rest of the marbles, including my blue taw.

Mama said, "We can leave this mess a bit longer. Let's all sit together on the couch, and we'll listen to the radio."

Mama and Daddy sat close together. Higgie climbed up onto Mama's lap.

Mama said, "You coming, Freedom?"

I picked up my beautiful sleeping sister and said, "Coming, Mama."

Stephanie J. Blake loves black jellybeans. She is scared of the dark. She reads lots of books. She's a terrible driver. She eats chocolate. A lot. Sometimes she has déjà vu, and she likes it. Her middle name is Jane. *The Marble Queen* is her first book.

When she's not in front of the computer, she can be found in her backyard in Colorado with her husband, their three boys, and their two dogs. If she weren't a writer, she'd be a country singer. Or maybe a pastry chef.

Visit her online: www.themarblequeen.com and www.stephaniejblake.com